Mary Vaughn Armstrong

Golden Gate Morning

LIFEJOURNEY BOOKS

Golden Gate Morning

LifeJourney Books™ is an imprint of David C. Cook Publishing Co.
David C. Cook Publishing Co., Elgin, Illinois 60120
David C. Cook Publishing Co., Weston, Ontario
Nova Distribution Ltd., Newton Abbot, England

GOLDEN GATE MORNING

Cover design by Koechel, Peterson, and Associates, Inc.
First Printing, 1992
Printed in the United States of America
96 95 94 93 92 5 4 3 2 1

Library of Congress Cataloging-in-Publication Data
Armstrong, Mary Vaughn.
Golden Gate Morning/Mary Vaugn Armstrong.
p. cm.
ISBN 1-55513-781-4
I. Title
PS3551.R472G65 1992
813'.54—dc20 92-47050
CIP

For my mother Helen, my sister Margaret,
and all the other nurses I have known and loved.

"Every good thing bestowed and every perfect gift is from above, coming down from the Father of lights, with whom there is no variation, or shifting shadow."

James 1:17, NASB

1

MORNIN', MISS CAROTHERS, I'm not in a huff . . . but wouldja please tell me where ya want this stuff?"

Kris braced her arm on the metal stepladder and smiled down at the only person in the hospital who spoke that kind of rhythm-English. Below her Nineveh cracked his usual wad of chewing gum, silently snapping the long fingers of one black hand as he gripped the chrome delivery wagon handle with the other.

"Nineveh, that's the seventh delivery this morning."

"Now we got pitchers, maybe six dozen . . . and I don't think they're for your cousin." With a twist of his shoulders, Nineveh two-stepped the awkward cart against the wall as the service elevator disgorged a nested stack of four gleaming portacribs.

Exactly where was she supposed to put it all?

Confusion pulsed through the MacKenzie Pavilion like a heartbeat gone wild. Unopened boxes teetered against the pale blue walls as yellow and blue vinyl chairs tilted beside them in precarious stacks.

For days Kris's staff had worked through lunch and coffee breaks and beyond, eager to put this move behind them by transferring their young patients from the old pediatric floor to the new. Everyone appeared to be under, on top of, carrying, pushing, or opening a cardboard box. They were dedicated and hard working, but they weren't miracle workers. And a miracle was exactly what they needed to be ready for the dedication by eleven o'clock the next morning.

Like a sluggish fish lurking in a shadowy pond, the old familiar fear surfaced in her mind. Kris swallowed, fighting against it. What if they didn't make it in time? What if the hundreds of details didn't all come together? She was the nurse manager, in charge of everything—but did she really have what this event required? What if she didn't measure up? Then what would happen to her job? And what would happen to Grandma?

The gum cracked again, sharper than before.

"Miss Carothers? I wait . . . you state."

"Sorry, Nineveh." Kris closed the storage cupboard and pushed her curly hair away from her eyes. "For now, just put them in the utility room, against the far wall. Maybe someone can unpack them later, when we set up individual units."

"We're on our way, 'cause this ain't play." Nineveh snapped his fingers and turned the cart around, his muscled shoulders straining against purple and pink suspenders.

"Kris?" Mandie's guarded voice drifted from one of the smaller playrooms at the far end of the hall. "Wait up. I need to talk to you."

Kris climbed down as her five-foot eleven-inch assistant nurse manager fast-walked the distance between them.

"Not more bad news, Mandie. . . ."

"Not yet—but I think it's coming." Mandie closed Kris's stepladder and braced it against a stack of boxes. "Sandy just stopped by from the main floor. The DNS is on her way up."

Kris groaned. Every person in University Hospital knew they'd been moving all week. Leona Steelman, the Director of Nursing Services, had to be aware of the pressure on the MacKenzie Pavilion staff. But maybe that's what her visit was all about. Pressure should have been Ms. Steelman's middle name, because she thrived on it.

The passenger elevator doors slid open and the DNS marched toward them.

"I'm outta here," Mandie whispered, heading for the utility room.

Kris smoothed her hair, wishing she hadn't splashed Betadine on her white overalls half an hour ago.

"Good morning, Ms. Steelman." Most of the hospital staff used first names, a familiarity scorned by the DNS.

"Hello, Miss Carothers." Hooded blue eyes swept the cluttered hall. "Operation on schedule?"

As always, Leona Steelman spoke in the military jargon absorbed during her twenty years with the Army Nurse Corps.

"The staff's working nonstop. I hope we make it by tomorrow."

"I know you won't let University Hospital down." Tight gray curls stood at attention over the ramrod straight back as Leona Steelman snapped open a black leather notebook. "I stopped by to inform you that tomorrow's dedication time has been moved up."

Kris felt sick. "You mean earlier than eleven?"

"We begin promptly at nine, so the doctors with noon surgeries can still attend. You'll be ready?" Ms. Steelman waited, her gold Cross pen poised over an outlined notebook page.

Kris's stomach growled loudly and she tensed her abdominal muscles against it, remembering the breakfast she'd skipped.

"We'll do our best, but—"

"Whatever it takes, Miss Carothers. I'm sure you're well aware that the new MacKenzie Pavilion is a milestone for University Hospital." A wispy smile skirted her pale face and disappeared as her veined hand punched the elevator button. The door jerked opened. Even the elevator didn't dare keep Leona Steelman waiting.

"Bye-bye, sunshine!" a voice whispered behind Kris.

She turned to see Mandie holding two Styrofoam cups of coffee.

"Thought maybe you could use this."

"Can I ever! She says the dedication's at nine tomorrow, Mandie. We'll never make it." Kris's eyes filled with tears and she looked away, leaning one shoulder against a set of cartons marked 5% Dextrose. "It's one interruption after another. I can't complete a single thing."

"Well, isn't this quaint. All you two need is some background country western, and you'll have your own little coffee shop!"

Kris didn't have to turn around to identify the speaker. No matter what Sybil Trefts said, she never failed to inject her words with several meanings. Today her auburn hair curled loosely around her face, a glowing frame for her flawless skin and exotic green eyes.

"This is the first time Kris has stopped all morning!" Mandie snapped, glaring down at Sybil.

"But things are pretty wild," Kris admitted.

Sybil was, after all, president of the MacKenzie Pavilion Auxiliary, a woman with an amazing talent for raising large amounts of money.

Sybil appeared not to hear either comment. "Have you seen Dr. Endicott? We can't wait any longer to finalize details for the dedication."

"He was here about a half hour ago," Kris offered. "I think he went up to the old unit to check on a few things before we start the transfer. By the way, did you know the dedication's been changed to nine? If you'd like to wait—"

"Nine? That's ridiculous. I must find him." Sybil's high heels clicked against the vinyl floor, the lingering scent of Boucheron perfume trailing behind her.

"Can you believe Garth Endicott was once engaged to her?" Mandie whispered, raising one dark eyebrow.

"No, I honestly can't." Kris sighed, glancing up and down the cluttered hall. She frowned, piercing her coffee cup's Styrofoam edge with one fingernail. Her eyes drifted to the sparkling white-capped bay framed by the east windows. The ever-present sailboats scudded across the cobalt waters of San Francisco Bay, while far beyond the Golden Gate bridge shimmered in the April sunlight.

She turned back to her friend. "Mandie, I've got every staff person I can spare up here from the old floor, but I'm not at all sure we can make it. Tell me the truth—with the dedication moved up, do you think we even have a chance?"

"I think we do. Sure, it's wild on the surface, but everyone's working hard, and underneath all the confusion things are falling into place fast." Mandie's expressive hands underscored each phrase. She drained her coffee cup and tossed it across the hall, landing it squarely in the center of an empty carton. "Believe it or not, Carmen's almost got the nurses' station organized."

Kris managed a small smile. "You always make me feel better. Let's go check things out."

They hurried up the wide hall and flipped on the light in the silent utility room. Pails, mops, germicides, cleaning carts, assignment sheets, and cartons of plastic pail liners had been stacked on shelves, every label right side up and facing out. Only Nineveh's boxes of water pitchers remained to be unpacked. "Mandie, you may be right. This place looks almost organized."

Next they inspected the supply room where labeled stock bottles, bandages of every size, prepackaged disposable tubes, stacks of sized oxygen masks, folded mist tents, and shiny new instruments lined the gleaming shelves. Looking almost comic beside the state-of-the-art medical supplies, a collection of cellophane-wrapped Ratty Raccoons overflowed a huge plastic bin. One stuffed animal would be given every small patient admitted to the Pavilion—children in need of all the comfort they could get. Behind glass doors the spacious overhead cupboards bulged with stacks of boxed disposable treatment trays. In the middle stood the med cart, already stocked with prepared unit doses.

As they left, Kris made a mental note that over a dozen cases of intravenous fluids still needed unloading.

"I'll get those put away before lunch," Mandie offered. "Need to inventory medications anyway."

"Inventory," Kris groaned as they hurried to the center of the Pavilion. The rectangular nurses' station was poised for action, its pale blue counters lined with neat stacks of intake and output forms, doctors' order blanks, all-hospital computer linkup, progress notes, lab and X-ray requisitions, medication and treatment Cardex, in-and-out baskets, all-hospital computer printout, call bells, central control monitor, telephones, and white plastic rectangles packed with pens and pencils.

Mandie and Kris found Carmen Martinez inside the station on her hands and knees, pushing backup stacks of printed material into a large corner cupboard.

Kris squatted beside the cabinet and peered inside. "Carmen, you've done wonders. Maybe there's hope after all!"

Carmen pushed a twelve-inch stack of lined white tablets in place and backed out, her smile contrasting perfect white teeth with her olive skin.

"One thing at a time," she said with a chuckle. "That's the key. I've been secretary here on pediatrics for eighteen years, and I'm here to tell you there's no other way to survive these things. Before you know it we'll be chasing kids up and down these halls." She slit open the taped edges of another box.

Carmen's words reminded Kris of her prayer before work that morning, a silent time that now seemed light years away. She had knelt beside her bed in the half-light, sensing the day's tensions, and one by one committed each hurdle ahead of her to the Lord.

The ringing phone interrupted her thoughts.

Mandie swooped to answer it, then covered the receiver and looked at Kris. "It's Dr. Endicott. Wants to remind you of the press conference at one o'clock."

Kris glanced at her watch. "I'll be there."

SHE HURRIED FROM THE ELEVATOR into the hospital's lobby at exactly five minutes to one, adjusted her clipboard and folder, and moved with long steps across the large and spacious entry. After polishing off a carton of blueberry yogurt, she'd stolen a few minutes to reapply what little makeup she wore, changed into a clean, pale blue uniform, and brushed her unruly blonde hair into a gentle if temporary curve at the back of her neck.

Looking poised and refreshed, Kris entered the conference room at the far end of the lobby. The large room's rich golden carpet and rows of folding chairs led her eyes to the long head table lining the far wall. Small clusters of people crowded everywhere, buzzing with excitement. Reporters juggled notebooks, videocams, and recorders as well-groomed directors of community agencies visited with curious representatives from local hospitals, churches, and volunteer groups.

Kris worked her way self-consciously through the crowd to the front table.

Ron Talbot, immaculate, controlled, and looking every inch the proud administrator of University Hospital, pulled out her chair.

"Thanks, Mr. Talbot," Kris said in a low voice. "This is quite a response, isn't it?"

"It's wonderful, Kris." He extended his hand to another arrival, his smile growing.

Kris leafed through her folder for a quick review, glancing up in time to see Dr. Endicott in the doorway. As usual his thick brown hair curled over his striped collar, looking as if it had been combed by a strong wind. A tweed sport coat formalized his slacks and casual shirt. It was impossible for Garth's six-foot-four frame to enter any room without dominating it.

He crossed to the front, pulled out the chair on Kris's left, sat down, and leaned toward her. "How're you doing? I'll admit I'm nervous."

"I'll be glad when all this business is over, and I can get back to running a pediatric floor." Something about Garth Endicott made it easy to admit the truth.

He nodded. As he leaned back in his chair, a bright red and yellow object caught Kris's eye. She stifled a giggle.

"Dr. Endicott," she whispered, "do you realize you have a Lego creation in your pocket?"

He grinned widely. "I sure do. It's from Tommy."

"Tommy Monroe? Our little guy with diabetes?"

"One and the same," Garth whispered. "He gave this to me before lunch. Strictly on loan!" He patted the awkward bundle bulging from his pocket as Mr. Talbot's voice rang through the conference room.

"I'd like to welcome each of you as we anticipate tomorrow's dedication of our new MacKenzie Pavilion. For all of us at University Hospital, ten years of planning are about to become reality. I know I speak for every one of us when I say this is a dream come true."

Chapter One

Kris looked across the room at Sybil Trefts, gorgeous in a light green blazer and white silk blouse. There was no way to tell if her intense concentration sprang from Mr. Talbot's carefully prepared remarks or Garth Endicott's magnetic good looks.

In the audience Kris saw a few people she knew. As she heard Mr. Talbot introduce Garth she swallowed nervously, surprised at her own anxiety.

"So it gives me much pleasure to introduce Dr. Garth Endicott, the Pavilion's outstanding medical director for the past year. I'm certain he'll be able to answer whatever questions you may have." Mr. Talbot sat down as Garth unfolded his long legs, cleared his throat, and stood.

"Thanks, Mr. Talbot. Hope I can live up to that. Now, what may I answer for any of you?"

Kris studied Garth's huge hands poised on the table's edge. So many times she'd watched them care with exquisite gentleness for the desperately sick babies and children on the pediatric floor.

A reporter rose to his feet at the back of the room. "Dr. Endicott, your father and your brother run one of the busiest private clinics in San Francisco. Why would you pass up an opportunity to work with them for a position that demands more and pays less?"

A ripple of laughter skimmed the room, followed by expectant silence.

"A good question—one I've asked myself more than once lately!"

The audience laughed again, less restrained.

"Yes, private practice is a distinct possibility. I'm sure I'll enter it eventually. But for now my interest lies in obtaining more experience in acute pediatric medicine, and in seeing one of the finest children's facilities in the state off to the best start possible. I might add that my family solidly supports my decision."

Good job, Kris thought.

A short, stocky woman stood up on the far right. "Doctor, can you tell us how many children are on the old floor, when they'll be moved, and how many the new Pavilion can hold?"

Garth hesitated, then turned to Kris. "I'm going to let Miss Carothers answer that, if you don't mind. She's been our pediatric nurse manager for two years, and knows those statistics better than I ever will."

Kris took a deep breath and stood, pulling her five-foot seven-inch frame to its full height. "To answer your question," she began, "the old pediatric unit has eighteen beds in all, counting babies and children. Our new Pavilion will have forty-four beds, including a four-bed neurology ward and a ten-bed pediatric intensive care unit. We'll also have eight rooms with live-in capacity for parents of critically ill children. Fortunately our case load is down right now, so we'll only be moving twelve patients tonight."

Another reporter stood in the front row. "We've heard a lot about the play areas—the supervision and extras available in them . . . even a room to care for hospital staff children who don't feel well. My question: how is all of this to be financed?"

Kris looked down at Garth, and again they traded places.

"Probably that can be best answered by the president of our volunteer Pediatric Auxiliary, Miss Sybil Trefts. As some of you probably know, Sybil's grandfather, Alexander MacKenzie, donated the original land for University Hospital." Garth flashed Sybil a warm smile, which she instantly returned.

"Some of the extra costs will be borne by admission fees, of course. But with the escalating costs of health care, University, like every medical center, needs additional resources," Sybil explained in her polished, well-modulated voice. "The Auxiliary Guilds have held five fund-raisers in three years, three annual house tours and two Christmas bazaars. All together they've raised well over three hundred and fifty thousand dollars."

A wave of applause swept across the room.

"We plan to continue these and more," she added, smiling broadly as the enameled "U Hospital 4 You" pin on her blazer gleamed in the overhead light. "We've used the money to purchase monitoring equipment and non-destructible toys and furniture for the play area. We look forward to contributing in a significant way to the special needs of the Pavilion." With another sparkling smile for Garth, she eased into her chair.

Kris arranged and rearranged the papers in her folder, imprisoned by the audience's endless questions and responses. Certain she would be up all night, like a bloodhound she mentally tracked the dozens of jobs still unfinished on the Pavilion.

Two and a half hours later, the conference ended with a burst of applause.

Kris jumped to her feet immediately. Going home was out of the question until she wrapped up all of tomorrow's details and saw every patient settled in the Pavilion.

Dr. Endicott buttoned his sport coat after glancing at his watch for the third time in ten minutes. "Kris, keep up the good work. I've got to run. I'll be back to check in later."

Every day, she thought. *I've known him a year, and he's left for two hours at the same time almost every single day. Why? And for what?* She watched as his blue-gray sport coat disappeared through the conference room door, a laughing Sybil Trefts in front of him.

Kris secured her folder and its contents to the clipboard, reminding herself for the hundredth time what a handsome couple Garth and Sybil made. Then she thanked Mr. Talbot, confirmed the upcoming transfer of patients, and hurried from the room.

At last the elevator arrived and Kris stepped inside, pressing the computerized panel for the eighth floor. She nodded at Dr. Freddie Burack, the only other passenger, then looked down. The straps of Dr. Burack's trademark Birkenstocks only half-covered his bright red socks.

Reportedly a brilliant if somewhat eccentric doctor, he had joined the pathology department of University Hospital three months ago. Though Kris tried hard to look for something positive in everyone, her search had failed with Dr. Burack.

"How fortunate can one man man get?" he murmured, crossing the elevator to stand beside her, his arm brushing hers. "All alone with the beautiful Miss Carothers."

Kris managed a thin smile and moved toward the door, staring fixedly at a microscopic spot on the elevator wall. His restless eyes and too-confident smile made her uncomfortable, and it seemed as if the eighth floor light would never flash red.

She squeezed through the doors the moment they opened, and moved quickly down the hall. Long after the elevator closed behind her, she could still feel Dr. Burack's probing eyes.

Her unease vanished as she approached the Pavilion. The responsibility for its opening, unquestionably the greatest challenge of her professional life, rested squarely on her shoulders. Gratefully she thought of Mandie, Carmen, and the many other staff members who had given a hundred and ten percent of their energy through the past grueling months.

Today they had outdone themselves. While Kris was waiting out the press conference, her staff had transformed the floor's mass confusion into a pediatric unit ready for action.

Though she heard voices of those still at work in the distant rooms, the halls were magically wide open and uncluttered. Even the cheerful blue-and-white sign reading "MacKenzie Pavilion" had been securely bolted in place.

Kris hurried toward it. For the first time in weeks she looked forward to tomorrow.

AT SLIGHTLY PAST SIX the next morning, Kris locked the dead bolt of her apartment door and turned into the cool April breeze blowing up Steiner Street. She hurried down the steps to the sloping sidewalk, fastening the buttons of her lavender all-weather coat as she went. The massive silhouette of University Hospital slumbered three blocks away, lights still burning in many of its windows.

Kris filled her lungs with the city's new-morning freshness, wondering if she would ever get used to its windswept beauty. Even at this hour the streets throbbed with rushing cars and people. She reviewed the day ahead and quickened her pace.

By eight o'clock last night she and her staff had finished their thirteen-hour day, the transfer of patients behind them. Within hours the Pavilion, now the city's finest pediatric facility, would be officially dedicated. She crossed the almost-empty hospital parking lot as the brilliant outside floodlights faded, and entered the quiet lobby.

CHAPTER TWO

AN HOUR AND A HALF LATER the Pavilion seemed to explode, the city's early morning luster a part of last night's dream. Kris watched as Carmen, rolling her eyes, reached for what had to be the floor's thirtieth phone call already. Seconds later she handed the phone to Kris.

"Phyllis from ER."

"This is Kris."

"I'm bringing up a seven year old, Kris. Couldn't do his addition last night, so his mother's boyfriend worked him over with a cast iron frying pan. Neighbors finally called the police. He arrived unconscious and has had three seizures already. The mother's disappeared."

"How far have you gone with treatment?"

"We've loaded him with Dilantin, phenobarb, and Valium. No seizures for ten minutes. He's had a complete neurological work-up including a CAT-scan. Didn't show any active bleeding, but he does have a possible basilar fracture. We put in a heparin lock and started a line of D5-1/2 normal saline."

"How about photographs and documentation?"

"They're finished—we're on our way."

Before Kris hung up the phone, the elevator doors slid open.

"We got daisies, and we got roses . . . and where we're gonna put 'em, no one supposes!" Nineveh sambaed around the cart that now carried four baskets of tall blue irises, white daisies, and yellow roses. He bowed, flashing a smile at no one in particular.

Carmen swooped to answer another call. "Three gallons of whole strawberries on the way up, Kris. Want 'em in the large playroom?"

Kris felt like a rubber ball bounced over and over against a wooden paddle. "One thing at a time! Carmen, notify Dr. Endicott stat. I'll contact Stormy in Intensive Care. Strawberries to the playroom—they can go right into the glass bowls. And Nineveh, I saved the best 'till last. Those flowers are beautiful!"

"They're from Patterson's Florist, Miss Carothers. . . . You want I should put 'em with the others?" Nineveh's brows arched high above his questioning eyes.

"Well, there's less than an hour to go. Just set them on the nurses' station counter. We'll distribute them in a few minutes."

After Nineveh sidestepped into the elevator, Kris headed for ICU. But first she stole a moment to bury her face in one of the bouquets, delighting in its cool, damp petals and springlike scent.

"You should try them with ketchup and mustard." Garth's warm, laughing voice caught her off guard and she jerked upright, her face scarlet.

"They kind of remind me of home," she stammered, feeling silly.

"Thought maybe you were on an iris diet . . . not that you need one!"

She ignored his comment, her mind on the little boy now on his way up. "Did Carmen reach you?"

"Not recently."

"ER's bringing us an abused child—he'll be here any minute. Doesn't sound good. I'm on my way to ICU."

Garth's hazel eyes darkened as he fell in step beside her. "Why don't you fill me in?"

He stared at the floor as they walked, absorbing every word as Kris repeated the little she knew of their new patient's brief history.

"Before he arrives," Garth asked when she finished, "how does it feel to be nurse manager on Northern California's most up-to-date pediatric floor?"

"Wonderful."

Garth cleared his throat. "Kris, after the dedication, would you—"

*C*HAPTER *T*WO

But before he could finish, a blanketed gurney sped past, propelled at either end by two orderlies and accompanied by Phyllis, one hand steadying the swaying IV bottle and the other bagging the ventilator taped to the child's mouth.

Kris raced after them, leaving Garth's unfinished question behind.

"Hi, Kris. First time in the new wing—this the right way?" Phyllis's face was grim.

"Just follow the yellow brick road," Garth muttered, his eyes on the motionless little boy strapped on his side to the narrow cart. He gripped its edge with one hand and half-jogged the remaining distance with the silent crew.

Kris raced behind them, assessing the gurney's unconscious occupant, noting the large ears under his matted black hair. Her stomach turned over as they transferred him with great care to a full-sized bed. Shiny purple-black swelling imprisoned both eyes, and a thin stream of blood trickled from the corner of the little boy's mouth.

"Dear God," she whispered, snapping on the wall suction before hooking up the ventilator.

"I want a skeletal survey stat," Garth ordered. "With a scan for old fractures."

"Here, little guy," Mandie whispered, tucking a Ratty Raccoon with white circled eyes under the covers.

Dear Mandie, Kris thought, *forever binding up the hearts of other women's children, all the time hoping and praying for her own baby that never comes.*

Stormy Ortner, assistant nurse manager of ICU, deftly positioned the sticky plastic surfaces of five white leads on the child's chest. "What's his name?" she asked tersely, pulling a pencil from her salt and pepper hair.

"Danny Kee," answered the ER nurse.

"Well, Danny," Mandie murmured, "this is Ratty Raccoon. He's yours to keep . . . and he loves you." Her voice choked.

Kris waited for the tears in her own eyes to clear before connecting the five leads to the heart monitor. Moments later, late for the dedication ceremony, she left Danny in the skilled hands of Stormy and her staff. As she hurried from ICU and passed the waiting room, she noticed a small Oriental woman huddled on the couch. The woman raised her head, her wrinkled face streaked with tears.

Kris stopped. "Are you part of Danny's family?"

Two wrinkled hands traced a helpless circle in the air as her small black eyes searched Kris's.

"No . . . English," she whispered. She held out a school picture of a black-haired little boy with big ears and a bigger smile, then looked away. The thin brown scarf stretched tight over her gray hair rocked back and forth in helpless resignation.

Kris poured a cup of tea from the corner table and handed it to her, making a mental note to check the file for someone who could assess what language she spoke. The hum of voices from the far end of the Pavilion intensified, pulling her toward it like a fish on a barbed hook. Kris patted the woman's thin shoulder and rushed on.

AT TEN MINUTES PAST NINE, she slipped into the second to last row of the folding chairs assembled in the large playroom. The restful navy, yellow, and light blue color scheme, carried out even to the staff uniforms, radiated cheerfulness. In the front row Kris spotted Sybil Trefts, elegant in an ice blue silk suit, gesturing with long, graceful hands in animated conversation with Mr. Talbot. Kris smoothed her blonde curls, wishing she'd at least had time to put on some lipstick.

At the far side of the room three television reporters jockeyed for filming positions. As the hospital chaplain concluded his devotional thought, Kris's eyes met Leona

Steelman's. Without moving her hands from her lap, the DNS rotated one fist, giving Kris an unmistakable thumbs-up sign.

Kris managed a smile, flushing at the uncharacteristic praise.

As Mr. Talbot launched into his address, Mandie suddenly materialized at Kris's side.

"He's had another seizure," she whispered. "Lasted five minutes. Garth's with him."

Kris gripped the edges of her chair. *How could someone do this to a helpless child? And why? Dear God, why?*

As Mr. Talbot continued, she forced her mind away from Danny Kee to concentrate on the present. Gratefully she spotted Nineveh's flowers, now attracting the rays of morning sun like invisible magnets.

"And so it gives me great pride, and a sense of deep responsibility," Mr. Talbot concluded, "to officially dedicate this pediatric ward as the MacKenzie Pavilion. May it be a beacon of hope to many generations in the years to come."

"And to Danny Kee this very minute," Kris whispered to Mandie.

Standing, the audience applauded and pressed forward to congratulate the administration and staff. As Kris followed Mandie to the refreshment table, she was surprised and pleased to spot Todd Franklin to one side, leafing through his pocket organizer. He wore the new brown sport coat she'd helped him choose from the rack at Macy's close-out sale.

"Hi, Todd," she greeted him. "I didn't really think you'd be able to get away."

Todd was an assistant minister at her church, and though though they'd gone out nearly every week since he'd come to San Francisco two years before, it was almost always to church or youth group functions. Neither of their schedules seemed to allow for much else.

"A meeting got canceled at the last minute. This is really something, Kris. You've done a marvelous job." They circled the long table dominated by a towering yellow and blue cake, a University Hospital replica created especially by the hospital bakery.

She reached for a plate. "How about something to celebrate?"

"No, thanks. We've got a youth training mini-seminar in twenty minutes." Todd glanced at his Seiko watch. "I set the alarm just in case, but I should get back. See you after church Sunday?"

Kris slid the clean plate back on the stack and stifled her letdown feeling. When wasn't Todd in a hurry? And why didn't he ever ask her to do something that took some planning? Then as always she felt guilty. At least he'd made the effort to be here, and she of all people should know the demands of his ministry never let up. "Of course. I'll look for you."

He gave her arm a friendly squeeze and left. Kris watched Todd cut through the crowd until he twisted left at the door to avoid crashing into a gray-faced Dr. Endicott.

Kris hurried toward him. "Danny?"

"He's gone." Garth stared up the ceiling, pain etched on his face. "This is the part I never get used to."

"What happened?"

"He broke loose with a massive epidural bleed . . . right on the floor. He never had a chance."

"And the boyfriend?"

"They arrested him at a laundromat this morning. Charged him with first-degree assault. Only now it's murder." He rubbed his eyes with two taut fingers. "Nobody knows where the mother is. There's a grandmother outside ICU. Speaks no English. I'll be off the floor for a while."

Garth plodded toward his office, his shoulders slumped with fatigue, and closed the door behind him. Kris longed to run after him, to comfort him with the only answer that could possibly make a difference. But this was not the time.

"Someday, Lord," she whispered. "He's hurting so much. Someday, please give me the chance to tell him about You."

With determined steps, looking neither left nor right, she sprinted past Garth's closed door back to ICU. As she entered, Stormy looked up from the nurse's desk. Together the two women walked into Danny's room. A pile of old sheets waited at the end of his bed. Beside them Ratty Raccoon lay face down on the mattress.

"Stormy, the old woman outside. Did you talk to her?

"I couldn't." She leaned against the mattress and rubbed the back of one wrist across her lined forehead. "We think she's Vietnamese. We're trying to find someone who speaks it, and we've sent for pastoral care."

"Does she know?"

"Dr. Endicott tried to explain, but—"

"Maybe I can."

A few moments later Kris sat down beside the tiny, forlorn grandmother, gently placed Ratty Raccoon on her lap, and shook her head. The old woman searched Kris's face, then clutched the stuffed animal against her chest, moaning in anguished, wordless grief.

3

KRIS SPOTTED AN EMPTY PLACE in the back of the dining room, boosted her tray to shoulder height, and worked her way between the tables. Nurses, doctors, technicians, operating room attendants in green scrubs, therapists, aids, and orderlies swarmed over University Hospital's twelfth floor Roof Restaurant. Surrounded on three sides by tinted glass windows, nearly every table overlooked the steep, tree-lined streets and houses of San Francisco.

She unloaded her salad-bar lunch and iced tea, grateful to be alone. Death shadowed everyone who worked in pediatrics, but the loss of Danny Kee had cut through staff morale like a band saw. Though the frenzied week that followed had dimmed that sad memory, the ever-present possibility of losing other patients remained an unspoken fear.

Kris bowed her head in silent thanks, then unfolded the letter she'd waited all morning to reread. Nothing cheered her more than a message from Grandma, filled with the homespun wisdom she'd grown up with.

*C*HAPTER *T*HREE

Dear Krissy,

They asked about you at Circle Group last week, like always, and about that nice preacher fellow. I explained that new pavilion place is opening, and how that you were right in the spot God put you, doing—

"Mind if I join you?"

Kris looked up, startled. Garth towered over her, tray in hand, ignoring the status of the doctors' dining room to his right. When she'd left ten minutes before, he'd been hunched over the nurses' station desk, penning entries into a foot-high stack of charts.

"No, of course not." She slid the letter into her pocket, suddenly apprehensive. Talking to him on Peds was one thing, but eating with him was another. They'd worked side by side for a year without so much as a coffee break together. Yet Garth hadn't been himself since Danny's death, and if he needed to talk about it, the least she could do was listen.

"I don't want to interrupt."

"Don't be silly! Please, sit down." She waved at the extra chair and marveled inwardly at the size of his lunch. A thick turkey and cheese on rye, full-sized dinner plate from the salad bar, big bowl of vegetable soup, potato chips, a glass of ice water, and a steaming mug of tea filled half the table.

"Your tea smells delicious. What kind is it?"

"Peppermint."

"You're not a coffee drinker?"

"I was born hyped up," he said with a laugh, squeezing a stream of honey from a shiny foil packet into the tea. "Fortunately, for once the Pavilion isn't hyped—it's almost quiet. But we've got three admissions coming in this afternoon."

"The lull before the storm?" Kris smiled. "It's hard to believe we moved only seven days ago, isn't it?"

His smile disappeared. "The credit for the success of that move goes to you, Kris. You had some great training somewhere. Here in California, wasn't it?" His eyes caught hers as he attacked his sandwich.

"Yes. AA from Yuba College in Marysville and BSN from Cal State, Sacramento. I graduated five years ago." She spoke rapidly, eager to be done with the small talk so he could unload about Danny.

"Then did you work there?"

"No, I went back home. Did floor duty in our local hospital for a year. It's small, so I got to do all sorts of things. It was good experience."

"And where's home?" he asked, offering her some potato chips.

"No, thanks. I grew up in Willows, north of Sacramento. You've probably never heard of it." Why was he asking for this boring history?

"I've heard of it," he said. "It's famous as a waterfowl refuge."

"Well, among other things. . . ."

"And why did you leave? I'd think a small town like that would make a wonderful place to live."

That surprised her. It was no secret Garth had been born and raised in San Francisco, part of one of its oldest and most respected families. He'd probably traveled all over the world, and she expected he'd look at small towns as nothing more than gas stops.

"It was. And I loved it. But my father was killed three and a half years ago. I needed to get away." She traced an imaginary circle on the table as her gray-blue eyes clouded.

"I'm sorry. You don't have—"

"No, no. It's okay. My dad had earned a living for his family since ninth grade by running the old family farm.

About forty acres of nut trees, a big flock of chickens, a dozen or so head of cattle. In his spare time he drove a school bus, to make a little extra. One day he was pulling out a stump, and the old tractor flipped over on him. He was killed instantly."

"I'm sorry, Kris."

His gentle hand covered hers, and she glimpsed around his eyes the tenderness she'd observed as he worked at a child's bedside.

"In any case," she went on, withdrawing her hand and forcing her mind back on track, "after a few months there was an opening for a staff nurse here at University. On Peds. It sounded like a challenge and change of scene, so I applied. I got the job, and began work on my master's degree at UC San Francisco. The nurse manager's position opened up two years ago. Guess I've never really wanted to do much besides pediatrics."

Garth listened, nodding from time to time. "And your mother?" he pressed.

Why was he asking her all this? But his interest seemed genuine, so she continued. "She died when I was five. I barely remember her. After her death Dad's mother came to live with us. She and Dad raised me," she concluded. "She still lives in Willows."

Kris's heart warmed as she thought of the ritual Sunday drives across the quiet town to church, Grandma's feeble attempts to help her with homework, and her endless admonitions to study, to learn, to prepare herself to earn a dependable living.

"She's still on the farm?"

"No, after we lost Dad we sold that. I don't have any brothers or sisters, so there was only Grandma and me to decide. We rented a tiny house for her right in town. She can shop and go places and visit a lot easier that way. And she's at church every time the doors are open!"

"I've noticed you always pray before you eat. I guess faith must mean a lot in your family." A new wistfulness colored his words.

Kris chose her answer with care. "It does. It's the most important thing in my life."

"It must be good to feel so deeply about something like that."

"It really is," she answered simply. Could this be the chance she'd prayed for? Then she glanced at the chrome wall clock between two floor-to-ceiling windows. "Oh, no. I'd better get back. Three more nurses still need to be relieved for lunch, and you know how the afternoon looks."

She slipped her purse strap over one shoulder, wondering how she'd ended up doing all the talking and wishing she could stay.

"Hold it half a second," he said, crunching on a piece of ice from his water glass. "I've got a great idea. You're still relatively new to our fair city—how about letting a real San Franciscan show you around? When's your next day off?"

"Well, tomorrow, actually."

"Perfect. I tried to ask you the day of the dedication, but there was too much going on. How'd you like to take a cable car ride with me tomorrow afternoon, and we'll have dinner at the best Japanese sushi restaurant in San Francisco?"

"Sushi? Garth, I don't know about sushi. Anyway, I really should—"

"Do the laundry?" The warmth in his eyes made saying no out of the question.

"I . . . it sounds very nice." She conquered the urge to ask him exactly what sushi was. "I'd welcome a chance to know the city better," she added matter-of-factly.

"Good. I'll pick you up about three-thirty. Where do you live?"

Chapter Three

"Three blocks from here, at 1230 Steiner. There's a sign out in front saying Oceanview Apartments, but you can't see any ocean. Just ring the bell under my name on the mailbox. I'll let you in."

"I'll see you tomorrow then."

"You may see me on the Pavilion first. After all, it's Friday afternoon."

Excitement rippled through her as she walked to the elevator. *He's a compassionate man who's kind to everyone,* she lectured herself on the way down to the sixth floor. *And he loves to show off San Francisco. Period.*

Half an hour later Carmen flagged Kris down by the nurses' station. "The little girl for an adenoidectomy's being admitted now. She'll be here in about fifteen minutes."

"Thanks, Carmen, I'll let—" The red emergency light for Room 624 flashed on and Kris flipped the intercom switch. "Desk, Miss Carothers."

"I need you down here, Kris. It's Tommy. I can't rouse him." Mandie's voice crackled with tension.

"Be right there." She snapped on Garth's intercom.

"Dr. Endicott."

"Garth. Kris. There's trouble with Tommy."

"On my way."

Kris heard the rhythmic squeak of his tennis shoes as he raced down the corridor, and almost ran into him outside Tommy's room. Amanda, tracking a blood pressure reading, didn't look up.

"When did you find him?" Garth muttered, one hand on the nine year old's damp forehead as he pulled each eyelid up, checking for level of consciousness.

"Maybe three minutes ago. Pressure's dropping. He's barely conscious." Mandie's hands trembled as she pulled her stethoscope from her ears.

"His color's terrible," Kris observed, closing her hand over Tommy's wrist for a pulse. "Skin's clammy."

"How about his glucose level?" Garth asked.

"Chemstrip was 130 at eleven."

"And now?"

"Two minutes ago it was 30." Mandie's brown eyes, always first to reveal her feelings, darkened with worry.

"I want an amp of D-50, 25 cc's stat." Garth ordered. "Then we'll move him into ICU until we get him stabilized. And get the lab up right away to confirm that Chemstrip. Are his parents here?"

"They were a while ago," Kris replied. "They've been taking turns sleeping in the room."

"Let's give 'em a call, Kris. I think we'll pull him out of it, but they should be notified."

Kris leaned toward the intercom. "Carmen? See if you can find Tommy's parents, would you? They need to get over here."

"Right away."

"Thanks. And let Stormy know we're moving him down to ICU."

After Mandie pushed the D-50 solution into the little boy's IV, the three of them wheeled Tommy's bed into ICU. Stormy met them at the door and pointed to a vacant room.

"Insulin shock," Garth said. "I want him on a cardiac monitor, oxygen by nasal cannula, and blood glucose readings every fifteen minutes."

Half an hour later Tommy's eyelids fluttered open. "Hi, Doc," he mumbled. He frowned as his half-open eyes searched the new room. "What's goin' on?"

"You took a long nap, Tommy. We'll tell you more about it tomorrow. You'll be in here for a while." Garth assessed the little boy's face and rumpled Tommy's sandy hair. "Feeling better?"

"I guess so. Where're my Legos?"

Chapter Three

"Right over there on the shelf by Ratty Raccoon," Mandie answered. "Ratty got sort of sleepy, too, but now he's feeling a lot better." She placed the stuffed animal at the foot of Tommy's bed.

Hurried footsteps announced his parents' arrival, their faces taut with worry.

"Tommy?" asked his mother, wrapping him in a careful hug. "How're you doing, honey?"

"Hi, Mom. Hi, Dad. I'm okay . . . but I'm hungry." He reached for his mother's hand.

"Mr. and Mrs. Monroe," Garth interrupted, "why don't you and Tommy visit for a while? Take your time." He clipped his ballpoint pen to the pocket of his plaid shirt. "Then both of you come on over to my office and we'll talk."

Halfway down the hall Kris caught up with him.

"Talk about frightening. Do you think we'll ever get that little boy's diabetes regulated?"

"He's a tough one, all right. Really brittle," Garth answered. "I think we've got him stabilized, and off he goes again. At this point his insulin requirements never stay the same one day to the next."

"Is there anything more we should be doing for him?"

"He's exactly where he should be. We'll get him regulated. But this summer he goes to diabetic camp. He and his family need to learn how to monitor his glucose at home, adjust his daily insulin, manage food exchanges, all of it. I want to discuss camp with them as soon as they come in."

As Garth entered his office and pulled out his comfortable chair, the tension disappeared from his face. "And tomorrow, Nurse, we forget medicine for a while!"

KRIS ROCKETED OUT OF BED on Saturday morning. Her fitful sleep had been shredded by a frightening dream—a nightmare in which Garth Endicott pleaded with her to find a missing lifesaving medicine packaged in a cast-iron frying pan.

She pulled on an old pink sweat suit and tied her hair back as she walked to the paned window for a weather check. Across the street, pansy-edged gardens greeted the thin rays of morning sun, reassuring her that the long night was really over. She could see her neighbors, the Petersons, having breakfast on their small brick patio.

Bill and Karen's friendly ways had quickly dispelled Kris's country notion that all city people were cold and indifferent. The day she'd moved into her apartment, Karen had appeared on her doorstep with a basket of muffins and a thermos of coffee. It felt good knowing they kept an eye out for her, and she tried to do the same for them.

She turned on the coffee maker, then one by one carried every houseplant in the apartment to the sill of the living room's large bay window.

"You guys take a sunbath," Kris whispered, stroking a pale new grape ivy leaf before placing a tiny pot of baby's tears beside it. Then she pushed a tape into the stereo and stretched her body through a rhythmic twenty-minute workout, hoping the exercise would reduce her mounting anxiety.

It was embarrassing not to know more about San Francisco, even if she did have night school and work as excuses. Why had she let Garth talk her into this? Well, it was just for an afternoon. In a few hours it would be a thing of the past.

She had almost warmed down with a series of slow body stretches when Mandie called.

"We're going running in the park, but I thought I'd check in." She hesitated. "Are you nervous?"

"Mandie," Kris scolded, "this isn't what you think. Garth and I are professional friends." She emphasized "professional," determined to cut short Mandie's matchmaking instincts. "He was born here in San Francisco, and he likes to see people get to know it. That's all."

"Call it anything you want, kiddo, but the way he's been looking at you lately shows a lot more than a chamber-of-commerce interest!"

"Mandie, he's serious about Sybil Trefts. Everyone on pediatrics knows it. And even if he weren't, there's no way he'd be interested in me. We're worlds apart!" As she talked, Kris cradled the phone against her shoulder and carried a red geranium from the kitchen table to the window sill.

"Believe that if you want to . . . but I remember how it was with Hank and me. My intuition says Garth Endicott and Sybil Trefts don't mesh."

"What do you mean? She was born in San Francisco, too—I heard they even went to the same private school. A year ago they were almost married . . . and he still meets her every single afternoon."

"How do you know that?" Mandie inquired.

"They're always together, and I saw them leave the press conference at the same time the day before the dedication. I think they'll be engaged again before we know it." Kris bent sideways, inspecting a tray of sprouting parsley seeds on the wooden shelf above the sink.

"She probably stays awake half the night dreaming up things to discuss with him so she can get him back!"

"Mandie, you're hopeless!"

"You're right. Well, looks like the other half of this romance is ready to go running. What time does Garth come?"

"About one-thirty." Kris felt her stomach turn over at the thought. "We're going for a cable car ride and to a sushi restaurant, and that's it."

And that, she made up her mind, really would be it. She'd get today over with and never think about it again.

"Anything you say," Mandie replied, "but I want to hear every single detail at church tomorrow!"

"I'll look for you. But don't ask me for details in front of Todd, okay? He's got enough to think about."

"I promise. Gotta go!"

Kris hung up, smiling in spite of her jitters. She poured a mug of coffee, then curled up on the blue and mauve cushion of her white wicker couch. How had she ever gotten through life before Mandie? From their first meeting as she combed the old pediatric kitchen for a can of Pedialyte, it seemed as if they'd always been friends.

Not long after that, Mandie and Hank visited her church and within a few months became members. From then on they'd been family in fact as well as feeling.

Kris sipped her coffee, admiring the rich green fronds of the Boston fern hanging in the sunlight to the right of the window. Then she opened her Bible, bowed her head, and asked God to bless the many things that must get done before she could let Garth Endicott set one foot inside her apartment.

It was past noon before she finished dusting, scrubbing the bathroom, and vacuuming the only rug she owned. After returning every houseplant to its place, she admired her tiny home. Grandma had always kept the shades of the old farmhouse pulled against prying eyes, but Kris felt proud, not ashamed. Her furniture might be sparse and secondhand, but beauty came from light and flowers.

There was still time for a whirlwind trip to the supermarket two blocks away. As she rushed into the apartment the phone rang, but the caller hung up when she answered.

Kris forced herself to drink a glass of milk, and set a Rye Krisp cracker and a thin slice of cheddar cheese on a paper towel. She propped an elbow on the smooth pine finish of her thrift-shop table, tried to eat and gave up, feeling more and more uneasy.

She showered and dressed, selecting a pink and brown vest hand-knit by Grandma. It would look good with her tan slacks and ecru pullover, a perfect combination for this bright, windy spring day. Tiny gold earrings and a single flat gold chain completed the outfit.

She pushed down her hair, which had been inspired by the shower's steam to even wilder curls than usual, and did a final check of the apartment. She spotted her thin photo album beside the couch and hastily slid it behind the bookcase. No reason for Garth to see that.

Her hands froze as the rasping buzzer invaded her thoughts. She pushed the security button and waited, chiding herself about behaving like a schoolgirl. Then Garth's footsteps sounded in the outside hall, and she opened the apartment door.

He dwarfed the doorway, more handsome than she'd

ever seen him in navy slacks and an Irish knit pullover covering a striped shirt. She met his eyes and invited him in, suddenly wishing with all her heart that she'd suggested they meet anywhere but here.

"Kris, this is great." It took him exactly three steps to cross the room to the bay window, where a ribbon of afternoon sun reached across the floor. "How long have you lived here?"

"Oh, a little over two years." She was surprised to find that her voice sounded halfway normal. "I learned about it by accident, through a nurse on another floor. When she moved out, I moved in. It's small, but it's affordable." She edged toward the door, eager to move the conversation onto less personal ground.

"You were lucky. It's next to impossible to find something this close to the hospital." He pulled a volume from the oak bookcase. "You have quite a library."

"I feel lost if I don't have something to read." She almost blurted out that she found most of her books at garage sales, then caught herself. "Uh, could I get you something? Tea, maybe?"

"No, thanks. I'm saving myself for sushi! What d'you say—shall we be off?"

Before his words were out she opened the door. "All set."

In less than a minute they were on the sloping sidewalk, a soft wind and the warm April sun on their faces.

HE OPENED THE PASSENGER DOOR of his maroon Audi for her, then circled the car, fastened his seat belt, and eased into the Saturday afternoon traffic.

"I guess San Francisco's famous hills don't bother you much," she said.

"Not a bit." He glanced over his shoulder and pulled

into the faster lane. "I learned to drive on 'em."

"That's one reason I haven't bought a car. I'm afraid I'll slide downhill and never stop!"

"It just takes practice," he reassured her. "How about our cable cars? They're well over a hundred years old. Been on many?"

"A few. Sometimes I take one downtown on my day off. I shop, buy some fresh flowers at a corner stand, and ride the car back home."

"Oh, yes. Flowers. As I remember, you have a real thing about them." He slowed to a stop in a left turn lane and shot her a teasing smile.

Kris remembered how he'd caught her with her face in the dedication bouquet and laughed despite her nervousness.

"I think this'll do it," Garth murmured, easing the car into a small parking area at the top of a tree-lined residential street. "We can park here for as long as we need." He let himself out, placing a small green receipt from the attendant on the dashboard.

"We'll catch the car here on Russian Hill. It's almost the beginning of the line," Garth said, opening her door. "They renovated the whole cable car system a few years ago. It should be a good ride."

He led her to a circled area in the middle of the street crowded with waiting passengers. In the distance the rhythmic, staccato clang of the cable car bell grew louder and louder as the car screeched and jerked its way toward them with surprising speed.

"It's almost like going back seventy years in time, isn't it?" she called above the noise. Venerable two- and three-story homes lined the street, their jewel-like lawns edged with spring flowers. Tall, luxurious green trees marched along the immaculate sidewalks, casting lacy shadows over the sunlit spaces between them.

"That's one of the things I love about this city," he

answered, his eyes on the approaching cable car. "Many sections do seem like another era, but at the same time it's as up-to-date as any city in the world."

As they talked, the Powell-Hyde line sped toward them, its brilliant maroon and gold paint shining in the sunlight.

"Booaard!" the grip man shouted.

Garth and Kris grabbed one of several polished brass uprights and jumped onto the car's lower step. A small Oriental woman pushed past them, gripping the hand of a little boy clutching a balloon, and disappeared into the glass-enclosed middle portion of the car.

"Fares now, please!" the uniformed driver shouted, moving toward them.

"Ever get tired of this?" Garth asked as he paid him.

"Wouldn't do anything else," he answered, reaching behind Kris to collect another fare. "This is the last surviving cable car line in the nation. People love it, and I can be outside having fun." He adjusted his brown cap and returned to the front of the car. The bell clanged again as he pulled a grip, and the creaking vehicle lurched forward on the track.

Kris grabbed the brass rail with both hands.

"You all right?" Garth laughed, slipping a protective arm around her waist.

She clung to the upright as the car gathered speed. "I'm glad I had a tight hold! These drivers don't wait around, do they?"

"Through wind, sleet, rain, hail . . . the cable car waits for no man!" Garth looked down at her. "Would you like to ride inside, Kris? It's warmer, and a lot easier on your hair."

"Oh, no . . . unless you do. I like the wind." She found a seat on the green wooden bench above the car's landing step.

Garth looked at her for a long moment, and she wondered what he was thinking. Probably realizing how unsophisticated she was, compared to Sybil Trefts. It wouldn't take a man like Garth long to figure out that she was confident in only one area: nursing.

Oh, well. He was generous to donate an afternoon to her, and she'd use those hours to learn all she could about his San Francisco.

But Garth wasn't ready to change the subject. "You actually enjoy the feeling of the wind?" he pressed.

"Sure. I quit worrying about my hair a long time ago. No matter what I do, it does exactly what it wants!"

Again he looked at her, the humming cables beneath the street magnifying his silence. "Your hair is beautiful, Kris," he said at last.

Something in his voice made Kris look up. But before she could answer, the bell clanged a warning and the cable car shivered to a stop in the heart of downtown San Francisco. Immediately package-laden shoppers, eager children, and map-wielding tourists swarmed over the tiny car.

Garth jumped off and extended his hand. She grabbed it, landing on the street just as the car lurched forward. The force of its momentum threw her off balance and again he steadied her, then led the way to the crowded sidewalk lined with restaurants and exclusive shops. She recognized the names of two elegant hotels, the Sir Francis Drake and the Westin St. Francis.

"Hungry?" He smiled at her. "The restaurant's about two blocks up the street."

She pulled her hand from his by pretending to adjust her shoulder purse. Together they worked their way through the jostling crowd of Saturday afternoon shoppers, making a wide circle around three street musicians singing "I Left My Heart in San Francisco" to an accordion accompaniment.

On their left stretched Union Square, one of the city's innumerable parks. Fragile purple and pink azaleas bordered its grassy expanse, a brilliant contrast to the gray stone wall behind them. On top of the wall, a noisy family of pigeons consumed a bread-crumb snack served by a bearded man in a patterned blue jump suit. Ten feet away a juggler tossed black and white rings into the air with dizzying speed.

"Those birds have probably never ventured more than a mile or two from here," Garth laughed, leading her around the juggler. "And why should they? They get their meat and potatoes served by hand, every day of their lives!

"And now, Miss Carothers-san, if you'll look up that little side street, you'll see the best sushi restaurant in San Francisco!"

As they waited for the light to turn green, Kris did her best to read the restaurant signs between passing cars. "What's it called?"

"Sakamoto's Sushi Bar . . . halfway down that narrow street near the corner. Black and white awning. See it?"

The light changed and they hurried across the street and into Sakamoto's. They walked into a low-ceilinged room energized by the hum of conversations from several dozen groups seated in front of a long sushi counter. As the pungent aromas of fish, steamed rice, spiced meats, and imported teas wrapped around her, Kris realized how hungry she was.

"Hey, Doctor—welcome!" A muscular Japanese man called to them from behind the counter, his chest encased in an immaculate white chef's coat.

"Sam!" Garth extended his hand. "Good to see you! Meet my friend, Kris Carothers. I don't think she's had sushi before. Kris, this is Sam Sakamoto, the owner and sushi master." He looked back at Sam. "I've given you quite a buildup. "

"I'm glad to meet you, Sam," Kris said, wondering if they served sandwiches.

Chapter Four

"You sit here," Sam urged, pointing to the long blue sushi counter. "I'm taking care of you myself. Right back. Thank you." His upper body bent forward in a brief, friendly bow.

Garth and Kris walked to two empty, armless chairs at the far end of the curving counter.

"Garth, what is all that?"

Behind the counter a motionless river of shaved ice held platters of food, much of which she didn't recognize.

"Those are all the things they use to create sushi. It's actually a vinegared rice garnished with everything you're looking at—sliced cucumbers, lemons, spinach, pineapple, seaweed, mushrooms, carrots, lettuce, daikon radishes—you name it. Sushi's really an art."

"And those other trays—is that fish on them?"

"Yes. Besides vegetables and rice, sushi uses all kinds of raw fish, like tuna, eel, octopus, sea bass, shrimp, flounder, sea urchins, and prawns, to name a few. Like to try some?"

"I . . . I'm really not too sure about raw fish."

"All fresh from the market this morning. What you think, Doctor?" Sam asked.

Garth hesitated less than a second. "Since she's a new sushi eater, Sam, let's try some California rolls. We'll each have a round of those. And a bowl of miso soup to start."

"Thank you—good choice," Sam bowed. "And maybe an order of tempura vegetables?"

"Garth, I don't know—"

"That would be nice."

"Some saki wine, Doctor?"

"How about it, Kris? It's a rice wine, served hot."

"No thanks. I'd prefer coffee or tea." He might as well know alcohol wasn't part of her world.

"No problem. Green tea for two, Sam."

"Good choice," Sam answered, bowing. "Thank you. You'll like."

"I hope so," she whispered to Garth, wondering what he had just ordered.

They watched as Sam positioned a large white plate, a six-sided white dish lined with leaves, a small red bowl, and three tiny black bowls on the preparation counter just beyond where they sat. "What is it we're having?"

"California rolls—seaweed wrapped around sushi, or rice, with crab and avocado on the inside. And simple vegetables in a clear sauce." He squeezed her hand. "The Japanese have been preparing sushi for over a thousand years. Trust me!" he laughed.

Moments later Sam reappeared with an intricately patterned teapot and two small cups, and carefully poured the fragrant tea. "Thank you," he murmured, bowing.

Kris watched Garth, wind-blown and relaxed as he handed her a cup of tea. Today he seemed so uncomplicated.

Be careful, an inner voice whispered. *His real life is the flip side of what you see.* Yet today's simplicity intrigued her, and she found herself wanting to know more about this man she'd worked with for a year yet hardly knew.

She sipped her tea and found it sweet and delicious. Sam noiselessly placed a small white and maroon bowl of steaming clear miso soup before each of them.

"I know you were born in San Francisco," Kris said, not wanting to sound too curious. "Had your family lived here long before that?"

"They moved to San Francisco in the early fifties," Garth replied, drinking his soup from its bowl. "Dad was in general practice, and the city needed doctors. Bruce and David were born earlier, in Nebraska."

"Your brothers?"

"Yes. I'm the youngest—a mere thirty-four."

"But you're all in medicine, aren't you?"

"Two of us are. Sort of in a rut, aren't we?" He smiled. "Dad and Bruce run a clinic near the hospital. I'll probably join them some day. David's a securities analyst."

"Why did you go into pediatrics?"

"I've gotta be around kids. Guess I really never grew up." His face grew serious. "Sometimes I dream of working in a place that doesn't have any medical care . . . maybe with migrant kids, or in a rural clinic."

"Where did you take your training?"

"Oh, in the East."

"Conversation stops now for first sushi dinner," Sam beamed. With polish and delicate precision he transformed the ingredients before them into colorful California rolls. Kris could not take her eyes off Sam's agile fingers as he tightly stretched thin black seaweed strips around an inner layer of glistening white rice that surrounded a blended filling of pink crab and pale green avocado.

He ceremoniously placed four inch-high rolls the diameter of a chocolate chip cookie on a bed of dark green spinach leaves arranged like a fan. Last of all he garnished each plate with a fresh yellow chrysanthemum. Nearby he set a white porcelain bowl mounded high with crisp, colorful vegetables in a shimmering sauce.

"Sushi dinner, thank you," he announced, smiling broadly. The production had taken over half an hour.

"Thanks, Sam. Better than Tokyo, as always!" Garth answered.

"This is a work of art!" Kris gave thanks in her heart for the elegant meal, wondering where she ever got the idea that sushi meant pieces of gray, straggly cold fish.

"But about your school," she continued, "did it have a name?"

"Well, first some graduate work in France. Then Johns Hopkins, and finally residency at Boston's Babies and Children's." He looked embarrassed.

"No wonder."

"No wonder what, Nurse?"

"You're such a fine doctor. I mean, that's pretty outstanding training. But it's not just the training. Healing is a special, God-given gift."

"Speaking of special gifts—" With a flourish, Garth took a bite of a California roll. "Superb!"

Kris followed his example and made a mental note to talk Hank and Mandie into a sushi dinner at the next possible opportunity. The contrasting flavors and textures of vinegared rice with mild crab and smooth avocado created an unforgettable meal.

"Garth, this is so good."

"Sam," he called, "another round of California rolls, please!" After a few moments of easy silence he leaned toward her.

"Would you like to do something else together tomorrow?"

His eyes were warm and expectant, but Kris felt herself pull away as her earlier unease flooded back. He was probably just trying to be nice. Besides, Todd would be waiting for her after church.

"Garth, thanks. This has been such fun. You've shown me a side of San Francisco I never knew. But I'm afraid I have plans for tomorrow."

"I thought you might. Church?" He did a good job of sounding disappointed.

"Well, yes, and then afterward I'm meeting some friends. . . . Do you ever go to church?"

"Well, sometimes."

"So you have a faith . . . in God?"

"For me it's impossible to study the human body and not believe in God," he answered firmly. "It's too perfectly put together."

"And Jesus? What about Him?" she persisted.

"I don't have that figured out, to tell the truth. Got a lot of unanswered questions." He stared at the motionless river of ice chips and its chilled cargo of vegetables and fish. "Jesus seems distant, sort of hard to understand, kind of long ago, if that makes any sense. I know it's not that way for you."

"No, it isn't. I'd like to tell you more about Him. Maybe you could visit my church some Sunday?" she heard herself asking.

"You name the Sunday. I'll be there." The speed of his answer caught her off guard. "I'd really like to understand more about this faith that means so much to you. And I'd like to know you better, Kris Carothers-san."

Kris lined up the finely hemmed edges of her blue napkin, wondering if telling him about her faith was going to be as simple as she'd thought. "That's important in any friendship," she said at last.

"Especially in this one."

What did that mean? Hadn't she made it clear that this was a warm but professional relationship? She looked away, longing to be home.

5

On Sunday morning a foghorn's mournful call woke Kris long before the alarm sounded. She stretched, savoring the rare luxury of extra time, drifting on the cottoned edge of sleep. Yesterday lingered in her memory like a welcome friend reluctant to say good-bye. She felt the warm breeze on her face, the pressure of Garth's hand on hers, saw the purple and pink azaleas against the old stone wall, heard again the laughter and excitement of shared discoveries.

"Enough," she said aloud, throwing back the covers. She walked to the window, yawning. During the night a silent fog had blanketed the sleeping city. Now a light mist fell, softening the geometric outlines of the apartments across the street. The clock on her bedside table urged her to hurry if she wanted to make Sunday school on time.

She enjoyed a brief prayer time by the bay window, showered, and slipped into a long-sleeved blue and burgundy plaid dress that would be welcome in today's light rain. As she reached for a tiny hoop earring, the phone rang. She dropped the earring and retrieved it from under the bed, but by the time she dashed to the kitchen whoever it was had hung up.

After a slice of toast and some orange juice, she stood in the living room and buttoned her coat. She could feel again Garth's energy as he'd crossed the small room.

But this was Sunday, a brand-new day. She gathered her purse and Bible and locked the apartment door, but after an invigorating half-block walk reached the corner in time to see the taillights of her usual bus disappearing down the street. Fifteen minutes later she caught the next one and enjoyed contrasting its bump-free ride with yesterday's clanging adventure.

"There you are. We thought you'd never come!" Mandie greeted Kris as she walked into the church's crowded all-purpose room, glad to be part of the friendly conversational hum.

"I was slow getting up . . . missed the bus," she admitted, loosening her coat belt.

"Can I hang that up for you, Kris?" Hank Dixon slipped his lined notepad under one arm and held out a lanky arm.

"Think I'll keep it on for a while. I'm still cold."

"The weather's a real change from yesterday."

"It was beautiful."

"What was?" Mandie handed her a cup of coffee.

"Thanks, Mandie. Yesterday was beautiful. But today is, too, in a different way."

"You can say that again. No handsome Dr. Endicott!"

"Mandie," Hank chided, "give poor Kris a break."

"Okay, but I want to hear every single thing!"

Kris sipped her coffee. "I saw a side of San Francisco I had no idea existed. Garth knows every inch of this city. We went to a Japanese sushi restaurant I'd never have found. Someday the three of us should—"

"How long were you together?" Mandie pressed.

"He came by about three-thirty and brought me home

by seven. The dinner's quite a ceremony—it lasted over two hours!"

"Did he ask you out again?"

"He wanted to do something today, only. . . ."

"Only what?" Mandie's voice jumped three tones. "Don't tell me you turned him down?"

"Mandie, we're friends," Kris said softly. "Period. It can't go beyond that."

"Why? Tell me why it can't be more than that." Mandie frowned, her large eyes puzzled.

A loud buzzer signaled the end of coffee hour and start of Sunday school, rescuing Kris from answering. "Don't we begin new classes today?" she asked, relieved.

"I think so. Which one are you going to?"

"I was thinking about the class on how to build up other believers." Even after four years in this church, Kris found it hard to choose from so many possibilities. Back home seventy-five people all together would have been a big turnout.

"Great—that's the one we're going to. I have to learn how to affirm Hank!" Mandie grinned at her six-foot husband.

"You don't need any lessons in that department." He grabbed her by the back of the neck. "That class is meeting upstairs, in the library. We'd better get going."

On the way up the stairs, Kris almost collided with Todd Franklin.

"Kris . . . hi . . . sorry!" He greeted Hank and Mandie, patting a six-inch high stack of Sunday school take-home papers. "Gotta get a slide projector for the junior highs and show the teacher how to use it."

He stepped closer to Kris. "How about lunch together after church?"

"We're going to Fisherman's Wharf for lunch," Hank said. "You two want to come along?"

"Great," Todd agreed. "I've never been there, believe it or not." He sped down the stairs. "Find you after church."

"C'mon, ladies," Hank urged.

They followed him to the library and found seats near the back. The teacher, a church elder who owned a downtown fitness center, asked them to turn to Romans 12:4 and 5. " 'Just as there are many parts to our bodies,' " he read, " 'so it is with Christ's body. We are all parts of it, and it takes every one of us to make it complete, for we each have different work to do. So we belong to each other, and each needs all the others.'

"Loosely translated," he added, "that means I need you and you need me."

So true, Kris thought. *But what if the person you need lives in a world light years from your own? Sure, people can change, up to a point. But basically you are what you are. Sometimes distances between people are simply too wide to bridge.*

Too soon Sunday school ended. Kris, preoccupied with the lesson, followed Hank and Mandie into church. In class they'd talked about ways to build bridges to people, and for some reason it had triggered a memory of the bleak Christmas before Grandma came to live with them.

On a gray December day, two women had appeared at the front door of their three-room farm house, one carrying a small turkey and the other a large box of food. Not quite six years old, Kris peered at them from behind the front room's faded wing chair, watching as their eyes took inventory of her home.

From that day on, she'd known they were different. Some families delivered food boxes. Her family received them.

After Grandma moved in, she drilled into Kris that it didn't do to get too familiar with anybody. Better to keep to yourself, she'd say. Better not to get too close.

And eager to please, Kris listened well and never forgot. . . .

They located three empty seats in a pew near the front of the church, facing the heavy wooden chairs where the ministers sat. Kris smiled up at Todd, seated to the pastor's left.

The rich tones of the organ blended with the piano's ringing chords, and the congregation stood for the opening hymn. "O Lord my God, when I in awesome wonder consider all the works Thy hands have made. . . ."

For the next hour Kris allowed the joyous words to vanquish the bittersweet memories of her childhood.

AFTER THE SERVICE SHE FELT a gentle pressure on her arm as the congregation buzzed its way into the wide central hall.

"Hi, Todd." She smiled, dropping a step behind Hank and Mandie. "All set?"

He shifted a stack of workbooks from one arm to another. "I'm afraid I need another ten or fifteen minutes to run over something with a teacher. Would you mind waiting?"

"Take your time." Kris caught up with Mandie and followed her and Hank to their car.

The minute the door closed on the Dixons' restored '57 Chevy Nomad, Mandie curled toward the plush back seat.

"All right, Kris. You said your friendship with Garth Endicott couldn't ever be more than that. I still want to know how come."

"Mandie," Hank cautioned.

"It's all right," Kris reassured him. "It probably does sound odd on the surface."

"Okay. You ladies talk. I want to know what '63 Chevys are going for. Time for a new project." He snapped open the *Chronicle* and disappeared behind it.

"It's kind of hard to put into words," Kris began. "I

don't know . . . it's just that I'm absolutely not what Garth thinks I am. I couldn't fit into his world in a thousand years."

"And what is Garth Endicott's world?" Mandie's graceful hands asked the question as much as her words.

"For starters, I learned yesterday that it's postgraduate work in France. He's fluent in French, Mandie! My family didn't even speak English right.

"His parents and brothers all had years of college. When my grandfather died, my dad was in the eighth grade. He had to quit school and go to work to help support his family. The Endicotts have traveled all over the world. I spent nearly all my life in a little town with three main streets."

Kris stared at the empty church parking lot, remembering.

Summer after summer, her childhood classmates took off in every direction for exciting vacations. Someone always asked Kris where she was going. One year, desperate to be like the others, she made up an elaborate story about a trip to Yosemite National Park. It almost worked . . . until one girl told her father and he mentioned it to Kris's father and soon everyone in town knew she'd lied.

"But, Kris," Mandie argued, "forget all that. You have a bachelor's degree in nursing. You spent five years in college. You studied microbiology and anatomy and a whole lot more. You can learn anything you want to!"

"You don't understand. It's so much more than education." How could she put into words how utterly inadequate she felt? In her mind she heard Grandma's blunt warning: *Water seeks its own level. And we're simple people. That's our level.*

"Well, what is it? Are you and Todd . . . ?"

"I can imagine marrying Todd someday. He grew up poor, too. He understands. Garth is involved with the opera, ballet, symphony, all sorts of civic functions. He could never be interested in the real me. I've never even listened to a whole opera, much less gone to one."

"So go to one! Puccini's *Madame Butterfly* is in town right now."

Kris laughed. "Mandie, I wouldn't know Puccini from pastrami."

Hank lowered his paper three inches. "Todd's coming down the steps, ladies."

"You're rescued," Mandie announced. "But I refuse to believe for one minute that you're not right for Garth Endicott."

Kris said no more as Todd opened the car door and sank into the plush seat beside her.

"Sorry to keep you all waiting," he said, loosening his tie. "Being a youth pastor requires about twenty-six hours a day!"

"Hey, no problem. Anyone for lunch?" Hank asked, easing onto Taylor Street. They drove past the landmark statue of St. Francis and soon spotted Fisherman's Wharf in the distance.

"I don't know when I like this city more, in the sunshine or in the fog," Mandie said, staring out the window.

"I'll take sun any day," Todd replied, stifling a yawn. "Fog makes me sleepy."

"Up late?" Kris asked as Hank parked the car.

"Roller-skating with the high schoolers. They wore me out!"

"Lunch should revive you," Kris said as they fell in step with the Sunday afternoon crowd ambling toward the wharf. "And you're about to get your wish—the sun's coming out." She pointed to a billowing bank of opalescent clouds. Parts of them separated, releasing long fingers of sunlight that stretched to the gray-blue ocean.

Chapter Five

"I'll never get used to the clean smell of salt water," Kris sighed.

Todd reached for her hand. "I've missed you, Kris."

"I've missed you, too. Don't think I've seen you since the Pavilion's dedication."

"I know. Guess my excuse is good news and bad. The good part is the youth program is growing by leaps and bounds. Kids are really hungry for the meaning and purpose Jesus Christ gives to their lives. But the bad part is that it takes more time every day. If I'm not with them, I'm planning programs and strategies for their next meeting."

"Todd, don't apologize!" Kris reassured him. "That's a terrific problem to have, you know."

"It is. Even now I've only got"—he gave his brown leather watchband a quarter turn—"a couple of hours before I have to set up for tonight's service. But it bothers me not to see more of you. Now that the dedication's over, maybe you can join me for more of the youth group activities. We make a pretty good team, you know." Todd squeezed her hand.

"That would be fun." They walked hand in hand behind Mandie and Hank, listening to the raucous calls of the sea gulls circling above.

Funny how different today was from yesterday. As always, Kris felt safe and calm with Todd. In the two years she'd known him, he'd never done one thing without advance planning. He mapped out everything on a meticulous written time schedule, from each day's "must-dos" to his life goals.

In her memory she heard Garth's spontaneous laughter as the cable car jerked forward and felt his strong arm hold her steady. But that was only an afternoon, and life wasn't lived on the crest of a wave. Todd was a predictable, safe harbor, comfortable to be with. And she could learn to be a good pastor's wife.

"Oh, smell that crab! I'm starving!" Mandie's laughter invaded Kris's daydreaming. The four of them stopped in front of an open stand, redolent with the delicious smell of oysters, fresh fish, and just-cooked crab from a boiling cauldron. Behind the glass counter a sunburned man arranged plump curled shrimp on a bed of chipped ice.

"Help you folks?" He waited, wiping his hands on a towel.

"Do you have shrimp cocktail?" Kris asked.

"Sure do. Caught an hour ago—take it to go and call it a walkaway."

"That's for me!" she laughed.

"Make that three shrimp cocktails," Hank added.

"Four." Todd smiled. "And let's get a whole Dungeness crab for the four of us."

"And maybe we can find a bakery for a loaf of sourdough bread," Mandie suggested.

Five minutes later they ambled by the Ripley's Believe It or Not Museum and several T-shirt shops, carrying cartons of shrimp cocktail, crab, soft drinks, and dozens of paper napkins. They followed the irresistible scent of freshly baked bread past seafood restaurants, a small recording studio, intriguing import shops, more fish stands, and arrived at last at a tiny bakery.

"This is it—hold it." Hank ordered. He bought a long, crusty loaf of hot sourdough bread and tucked it under one arm. "We'd better land somewhere—I can't resist this for long."

"There was a little park near where we left the car," Kris remembered. "I'm almost positive—I remember the flowers."

Mandie laughed. "If she remembers flowers, there were some. Let's go!"

They retraced their steps along the wharf and soon discovered a small, grassy area edged with cream and orange daffodils, complete with a weathered cedar table and two benches. Mandie and Kris arranged the picnic on the table, using the crab's white wrapping paper as a tablecloth. They distributed plastic spoons and forks, then placed the warm bread in the middle of the feast.

"Okay, Todd, you're the clergy here. Would you give thanks?" Hank asked.

Todd bowed his head. "Lord, thank You for this day, this food, and for good friends. In Jesus' name. Amen.

"I meant that . . . especially the part about food!" He laughed, pulling a narrow piece of white meat from a crab's leg. "But mostly I'm glad we're all here together."

"So the youth program's growing, Todd?" Hank stretched his long legs and leaned against the bench.

"It sure is. I was just telling Kris how the kids are really hungry for meaning in their lives. They come from every kind of background, but they all share the need to know Jesus' forgiveness and plan for their lives.

"Like Angela," he continued. "She showed up about two months ago, from a home situation you wouldn't believe—just about every kind of abuse going on. She's committed her life to Christ, and now three of her friends are coming to youth group with her. She still has lots to work out, and it will take years, but she's on her way. I don't need to tell you it's exciting. But it's also the biggest challenge I've had in my ministry so far."

"You were in Merced before you came here, right?" Hank tore off a piece of French bread. "Isn't that near Yosemite?"

"Yes to both questions. I was in Merced for three years—right after seminary. Sort of cut my teeth there, and it prepared me for this ministry in a real way. But I never expected this kind of growth, or to deal with so many kids at once."

"I can identify with that," Hank said. "Sometimes I look

at my class and wonder how one teacher can be effective with forty kids at once, half of them from dysfunctional homes."

"Are you still teaching fifth grade?" Todd asked.

"Yes. It's a great age. Ready for challenges, but minus the complications of adolescence."

"Help! Who's got the napkins?" Mandie cried, licking her fingers.

"Here, tuck one under your chin," Hank joked, handing her a stack of napkins. "Oh, Mandie, look!" he said, pointing.

A rainbow-colored plastic ball rolled toward their bench, followed by a staggering, smiling baby about a year old. Dressed in jeans and a baseball cap with the brim turned backwards over his chubby neck, he looked like a miniature first baseman.

"Oh, Hank, he's adorable!" Mandie knelt down and placed the colored ball between the baby's outstretched hands. As he waddled away, his barefooted, blue-jeaned mother scooped him into her arms and disappeared over a small rise of grass.

Hank and Mandie watched them leave.

"Someday, honey . . . someday," he said, and his words were very gentle. "Our turn's coming. . . . . Now what can I get you? Some of that great bread?"

Kris and Todd quietly finished lunch while Hank wrapped his arms around Mandie and held her close. Mandie gave so much of herself to everyone around her, but the heartache of her infertility never left. Every day Kris prayed that her best friend's chronic endometriosis would end with the new drug she'd been taking the last two years.

"Anybody for a walk along the waterfront?" Hank said at last, breaking the long silence. "I'd like to see that old sailing ship again. What's its name?"

Chapter Five

"The *Balclutha,* I think you mean," Todd replied. "It's got an iron hull. I've read that it's really beautiful."

"I'd love a walk." Kris jumped up.

They dropped their papers in a trash can and strolled past sailboats and drying nets to the pier where the graceful old ship was moored.

Kris and Todd walked slowly, listening to the lazy, creaking sounds of the colorful fishing boats anchored on either side. The chilly fog bank still hung over the shimmering bay, but on this slender pier the sun felt soothing and warm.

"It seems so right being with you, Kris," Todd said in a low voice. "I wasn't just talking when I said we make a good team." His blue eyes searched hers, his face freckled and boyish despite his twenty-nine years. "Before long I'd like to make that permanent," he said tenderly, his arm tightening around her waist. "When my great-uncle died, my great-aunt gave me her ruby engagement ring. I'd like to put it on your finger someday, Kris. What would you say to that?"

The sweetness in his voice touched her heart. Nothing, she knew, would make Grandma happier than to see her married to a pastor.

Hank and Mandie were far down the wharf, alone with their longing, the circling sea gulls the only living creatures nearby. Kris felt Todd bend to kiss her, and turned her face away.

"Todd, I'm sorry."

"What's wrong, Kris? You know how I feel about you, that someday. . . ."

"It's just . . . I guess I need some time."

"You have all the time in the world. You know that."

As they walked on, she tried to make sense of her feelings. Todd was like her in so many ways. His missionary family had moved often and had few luxuries. Like his father, Todd's greatest passion in life was telling people about Jesus. His work with young people had eternal meaning, and she could see herself someday working beside him in the ministry.

Still something nagged at her, held her back, something she couldn't identify. She was ashamed to find herself wondering if he'd outlined his plans to marry her on his long-range schedule. . . .

YOU'RE COMING AROUND, aren't you, Tina-girl?" Garth murmured to the small mountain of white blankets in the middle of the ICU crib. "Pass me a tongue blade, will you, Kris?"

She pressed the slender stick into his hand, focusing on the reassuring beep of the cardiac monitor.

Garth rechecked neurological reflexes, taking extra care to keep the thermal blankets tucked around their unconscious patient. Inside her white cocoon, resting on a heat mattress and still shaking, slept eighteen-month-old Tina Salazar. Little by little, the child's pulse grew stronger and her bluish skin hinted at a healthy pink.

"Tell me again how this happened," Garth said, checking Tina's foot reflexes.

"When Phyllis brought her into ICU, she said Tina's family was camping in the Sierra foothills," Stormy Ortner answered. "Early this morning Tina wandered away and fell into a creek. Even in May, the water's still freezing. From what her mother said, she was submerged for ten or even fifteen minutes."

Stormy rechecked the pump administering intravenous medication to raise Tina's critically low blood pressure. "When they found her she was blue and not breathing. The first core temp the paramedics got was eighty-eight degrees."

Garth nodded. "In that kind of cold the body basically shuts down everything but essentials. The person looks and feels dead, but with aggressive care they can survive. Tina's in critical condition, but she'll make it. The bottom line is somebody didn't give up."

"Her mother says it was a miracle," Kris added. "I think she's right."

"She may be. Storm, we'll rewarm her as fast as possible. The monotherm probe's in place?"

"Yes. We've got a continuous basal temp readout."

"Good. Constant thermal blankets and hot packs. Notify me immediately if she changes."

"Yes, doctor. Anything else?"

"We'll start warm drinks when she's fully conscious and keep her right here in ICU until she's stabilized. Then we'll still watch her for a day or two." Garth folded his stethoscope.

"I'll let her parents know," said Kris.

"Excuse me, Kris." Carmen stood in the doorway. "Pathology just called. Someone will be up in fifteen minutes to examine LeRoy Jones. Anything special you want me to get ready?"

"Not at this point, Carmen, thanks. I'll be right out."

"Okay. And, uh, Dr. Endicott, Miss Trefts is waiting in your office. Something about wallpaper strips."

"I'm coming." Garth stuffed the stethoscope into the back pocket of his blue corduroys and started for the door. "You going, Kris?"

"In a few minutes. Stormy and I need to run over some things." The excuse sounded natural enough to her own ears, and she hoped it did to Garth and Stormy. Carmen's words had set off fresh waves of apprehension, and she needed a minute to get hold of herself.

Since the Pavilion opened, Sybil Trefts seemed to show up at all hours of the day on what she described as "auxiliary business." Whatever it was, she walked behind the desk too often, listened to too many conversations, knew too much about the patients.

After a final review with Stormy, Kris left the ICU. On her way back to the nurses' station she couldn't help seeing Garth and Sybil standing close together at the end of the hall, laughing. Impeccably groomed, Sybil wore a snugly belted khaki dress that left little of her beautiful figure to the imagination. As Kris turned the corner Sybil laughed again, tipping her head back and playfully shaking her long auburn hair.

Kris sank into a chair to review LeRoy Jones's chart, weary and feeling anything but glamorous. From the moment Tina arrived by emergency air transport, she had been intensely involved in the little girl's care and knew she looked it. Her hair and lipstick hadn't been touched since she came on duty, and her once-immaculate uniform was smeared with mud from Tina's clothes.

She skimmed the record detailing LeRoy's care, forcing herself to concentrate. Six years old, he'd been admitted two days ago for evaluation of anemia, persistent fever, unexplained fatigue, and greatly enlarged lymph nodes. Differential diagnosis included a strong possibility of malignancy. This morning a node biopsy had been done, and the detailed physical exam would help make the final evaluation.

"Miss Carothers? Dare I hope you'll help me examine the Jones boy?"

Dr. Burack leaned far over the nurses' station counter, staring just above Kris's head at the wall behind her.

She forced an answer. "Hello, Dr. Burack. I'll show you to LeRoy's room. Is there anything special you need?" She waited a moment for his response, then started down the hall.

"Everything I need is right here," he said, falling in step close beside her.

His tone repulsed her, and she wondered where the hospital had ever found this strange man. As they entered LeRoy's room, she focused her attention on the sallow, wide-eyed boy sitting cross-legged in the middle of his bed.

"This is the patient?"

"Yes. His name is LeRoy."

Dr. Burack's eyes narrowed. "So be it . . . LeRoy. I'm Dr. Burack, and I need to examine you. Lie down, please."

How could anyone, most of all a doctor, fail to see how feverish and obviously frightened this little boy was? Kris tried to reassure him with a smile, turning his pillow over so the cool side was under his neck and head, then tucking Ratty Raccoon beside him.

"When was the biopsy done, and what does the specimen look like?" Dr. Burack mumbled as he peered into LeRoy's throat.

Kris's face flushed with anger. "I think it's best if we discuss that out of the patient's range, Doctor," she said in a low voice.

"Miss Carothers! Surely you don't think this small boy could possibly under—"

"He understands every word. I have all the information you need, after you've finished. How're you doing, LeRoy?" She managed a smile, searching her pocket for her scissors to trim the frayed bandage on LeRoy's Ratty Raccoon. She checked her other pocket, then a third, and made a mental note to ask Carmen if she'd seen them.

"I'm okay, Miss Carothers. But you'll stay, won't you?" LeRoy's hot hand gripped Kris's.

Chapter Six

"She has no choice, LeRoy," Dr. Burack smirked, glancing sideways at Kris as he palpated the little boy's stomach. "Those are the doctor's orders."

Kris wanted to run out of the room.

"Everything okay in here?"

She welcomed Garth with a relieved smile. He glanced from Kris to Dr. Burack, who was slowly pulling his stethoscope from his neck.

"Fred, why don't you join me in my office when you're through? I'll brief you up to this point. LeRoy's a pretty special guy around here!" He rumpled the child's curly hair, and the little boy's face lit up, revealing two missing front teeth.

"I'm finished now, Doctor," Dr. Burack replied stiffly.

"Good. Kris, we'll leave you to settle LeRoy. Fred, there are some details here you'll want to know, to balance off—"

LeRoy's door closed behind them. Kris, amazed at Garth's skill in maneuvering Dr. Burack out of the room, challenged LeRoy to a game of tic-tac-toe on his new magic slate.

Hours later she stretched as high as she could on the tips of her toes, enjoying the release of tension the motion brought her aching leg muscles. The view from the utility room window always relaxed her as she absorbed the beauty of the twinkling city below. She yawned, thinking wryly of her nursing arts instructor's admonition that "professionals don't count hours."

"Kris! You still here?"

She turned from the window as Garth entered the room. "Hi. I thought you and Sybil took off hours ago."

"We went in separate directions. I came back awhile ago to recheck Tina and a few others."

"How's she doing?"

"Pretty well. Temperature's almost up to normal and she's stopped shaking. How about you? Haven't been home yet?"

"Well, no. I had to schedule staff hours for June and make some changes in the Pavilion tour protocol. But I'm ready to call it a day."

"Had dinner?"

"Yes. Went up to the Roof about five."

"Well, then . . . could I walk you home?"

"Oh, that's all right. It's only a few blocks. I'll be fine."

"As close as you live, you still shouldn't be walking alone at night. Let me look in on LeRoy and I'll be finished. Okay?"

Kris nodded, too tired to resist. Garth sounded like her neighbor, Bill Peterson. But Bill was a retired cop, and thirty years on the beat had probably taught him to expect the worst. Well, company for the three-block walk would be welcome.

"That'd be nice, thanks," she replied. "I'll be at the desk."

Ten minutes later they walked through the hospital's sliding glass doors, and Kris shivered in the cool evening air.

"I've been inside too long," she laughed, buttoning her coat. "Real air feels cold!"

"You had a day of it, didn't you?" Garth asked as they climbed the steep sidewalk toward her apartment. "And I gather Dr. Burack didn't win any points with you, either!"

Kris frowned. "There's something about him. He never takes anything the way it's meant. And his attitude toward little LeRoy was disgusting. He talked to that boy as if he were a piece of meat." Thinking about it made her angry all over again.

"Whoa! He's back in pathology, I hope to stay for awhile." Amusement edged Garth's soothing words.

"Wherever he took his medical training, I think he

missed the part about respecting how children feel."

"Maybe that's why he's in pathology—cells don't talk back!" They crossed the street. "He never comes to any of the staff get-togethers, so I hardly know him. But he's one of the best pediatric pathologists in the country."

"I'm still glad you came in when you did. I don't like being alone with him, even with a patient there. He's . . . I don't know. . . ."

"I understand. And I'd just as soon you weren't alone with him, either. On a pleasanter subject, I believe this is your apartment, Miss Carothers."

"I hate to stop—it felt good to walk." Below them the lavender dusk had yielded to darkness. "Would you like to come in for a few minutes?"

"I'd like that very much."

Kris walked quickly through the dark apartment switching on lights. In the sudden brightness the rows of books, graceful splashes of green plants, and the room's soft colors seemed to come alive.

"You have a real knack for making a place relaxing," Garth told her.

"Thanks. It's small, but it's home and I love it. I don't think I've ever asked where you live."

"I have an apartment in the Marina. Nothing fancy, but I have a great view of the Bay. That was important."

"And it's one thing that's missing here," she said with a laugh. "How about a cup of tea?"

"Sounds good." He followed her into the kitchen and sat down, eyeing the red geranium resplendent with two new flowers. "You must have inherited your father's green thumb."

"Sometimes I think so," Kris answered. "I never get tired of puttering in the soil."

"What about your manicure, Nurse?"

Kris laughed, too tired to worry about what he thought.

"I guess that's like my hair—I try not to worry about it!" She set two mugs of peppermint tea on the table, and in Garth's eyes recognized the same peculiar look she'd seen on the cable car.

He smiled. "Peppermint tea!"

"Yours smelled so good in the cafeteria the other day that I had to buy some. After a day like today, I need something to relax."

"Know what you mean. It never calmed down." He hunched forward, circling his mug with both hands. "I've tried to find a way to leave it behind me, but sometimes that's pretty hard to do."

"Like LeRoy?"

"Like LeRoy. He's a very sick little boy, I'm afraid. The tests don't look good."

"I suspected that. I'm not preaching, Garth, but dealing with situations like LeRoy's is one place where my faith really helps. Without it, I don't think I could handle some of the heartbreak on pediatrics."

"But I can't switch off my brain, Kris. I studied all that stuff, but for some kids all the statistics and drugs and facts only add up to a big fat zero. To see a child—an innocent child—face death, and his own doctor can't do a thing. . . ." The muscles around his mouth tightened.

"You're trying to carry it all by yourself, but it won't work. Sooner or later it'll pull you under."

"I've got a feeling you've been through some deep waters yourself."

"When I lost my dad, I thought the end of my world had come. Maybe having so little all those years made us closer. Dad always worked so hard for us, but things never seemed to go right. I'd always hoped I could help make it easier for him." Kris looked down. "When he died, I felt lost . . . totally alone. But I still had Grandma. She kept at me to get back to reading my Bible. One night, mostly to please her, I read straight through the Gospel of Matthew. When I finished, something had happened to me. I knew I'd never, ever be alone again."

"How can anyone possibly know that?"

"Well, it's in the last verse of the last chapter, where Jesus is talking to His disciples. He tells them to go into all the nations and make more disciples, and He says, 'And be sure of this—that I am with you always, even to the end of the world.' "

"That is powerful."

"It's the 'always' that got to me," Kris said, her voice intense. "God showed me that 'always' meant in any and every circumstance. In the loss of my dad, and in never knowing my mom, and in always feeling so . . . so different from other people. And in the small things too, like too many bills and never enough money."

"Does He promise that for everyone?"

"Well, yes and no. It's for everyone who believes in Jesus . . . everyone who's one of His followers."

Garth was silent. "Is it hard to follow Him, Kris?" he finally asked.

"Oh, no! He even says that His yoke is easy, and His burden is light. He doesn't say His followers won't have problems and sadness, but when those things come He promises to be right there in the middle of it with them."

Kris's heart leapt as she saw the depth of emotion etched on Garth's face.

"But . . . when does all this happen? When you join a church? I'll be frank, Kris. To me religion has always seemed like a sort of righteousness slot machine. Put in prayers and church, get back a gold star."

"But this isn't religion. I'm talking about a relationship with Jesus first, above everything else. He's always there, like a best friend. Joining a church comes later." She prayed silently for the right words.

"To follow Jesus," she continued, "all that's needed is to be honestly sorry for everything we've ever done that's hurt God. The Bible calls those things sin. We need to confess those to Jesus, and then turn to Him as Savior and Lord. When we do that, the Bible tells us He forgives us everything, and makes us His children."

Neither of them spoke for several minutes as the scream of an approaching siren and a cargo ship's mournful call drifted through the kitchen window. As the sounds faded away, Kris touched his arm.

"Garth, do you have a church?"

He looked at her and she sensed he'd been miles away in thought.

"Well, I guess you could say so. I don't go very often."

"Mine's not far from here. Would you like to come next Sunday? There's a class at nine-thirty, church at eleven. You don't have to go to both, unless you want to."

"I'd like that. I need to make rounds first, so maybe I'll come at eleven. You'll be there?" This time he was the one sounding nervous.

She smiled, eager to reassure him. "I'll be there. Mandie Dixon and her husband, Hank, go too. Maybe we can sit with them."

As they stood at the door of her apartment a few minutes later, Garth looked down at her, saying nothing. Then he took both her hands in his, leaned forward, and gently kissed her cheek.

Kris stared up at him, bewildered.

"You don't know what this talk's meant to me," he said, his voice gruff with feeling. "Sometimes it all piles up. I realize how little I know, how little I can do. Tonight you've given me a glimpse of some answers. I'm looking forward to Sunday."

Kris closed the door and leaned against it, too happy and too tired to think.

7

THE SUPERVISING NIGHT NURSE'S voice droned from the tape recorder centered on the report room table. "LeRoy Jones, Hodgkins disease, began chemotherapy four days ago. He spiked a fever of 104 around one a.m. . . . spent a pretty rough night.

"Tina Salazar slept straight through. Here four days and going home, good as new.

"Sam Bennellick was admitted during the night, doubled over with abdominal pain. Had an appendectomy about three hours ago.

"Karen Scavone rested. . . ."

The day shift clustered around the small machine, listening for every detail as the first tentative rays of morning sun probed the walls of the small room. Given by the outgoing shift to those coming on duty, the report provided a litany of the preceding eight hours, a time-honored and vital link in consistent patient care. As the staff scribbled notes, the smells of Betadine and strong coffee hung in the warm air.

Kris stood next to Ruby Cates, the night shift's hollow-eyed nurse manager, absorbing every detail. Experience had taught them both that the complexion of an entire floor could change without warning during long nights of illness. As Kris heard the update on LeRoy, she was glad Garth's visit to her church was only two days away. There were times in medicine when knowledge, however current, was simply not enough.

When the last patient's status had been described, Ruby turned off the recorder and pulled the stethoscope from her neck. "Before you get your individual assignments," she said, folding the rubber tubing to a narrow oval, "I want to remind all of you about the annual staff picnic."

Kris felt the group relax as they caught the enthusiasm in Ruby's voice.

"It's the night shift's turn to plan it," she continued, "and we guarantee the best ever! Spread the word, because everyone's invited: nurses, ward clerks, housekeeping staff, volunteers, doctors, everyone. The date is Saturday, May 30, two weeks from tomorrow, at the Children's Playground, Kennedy and Bowling Green Drives, in Golden Gate Park.

"The picnic starts at one, rain or shine. Do whatever you want—ride horseback or bike, hike, roller skate, play tennis, shoot archery, golf. Or none of the above. We end around six with a big barbecue. Night shift provides hamburgers and trimmings. The rest bring a big salad if your last name starts with A through L. M through Z, bring a big dessert."

Everyone knew Ruby Cates threw herself into whatever she did. She'd worked nights at University Hospital for twenty years and had a reputation for demanding the best from everyone, including herself.

Kris watched the staff disperse, making plans for the picnic as they hurried to review the Cardex and discuss detailed patient care assignments with the outgoing night nurses.

"Thanks, Ruby," she said with a smile. "See you on Monday. I promise to schedule off everyone I can spare for the picnic."

The next few hours sped by in a flurry of medications, treatments, baths, reassurance, new orders, hugs, admissions, and discharges, accompanied by phones that never stopped ringing.

"Kris, you better take a break while the gettin's good—lunchtime's not far off," Carmen warned, catching Kris between calls.

"Thanks. I could use a cup of coffee. Dr. Baker just ordered a CAT-scan on little Evangeline Prince as soon as possible. Could you arrange for that? And Carmen, I meant to ask—have you seen my scissors? They've disappeared."

"Your name on them?"

"Inscribed on the inside." There was nothing unusual about the stainless steel bandage scissors with the blunt, bent edge, but Kris ascribed a high sentimental value to them because they'd been Grandma's nursing school graduation gift.

"Haven't seen 'em," Carmen said, "but I'll keep an eye out. Now, what about that break?"

Kris walked down the hall and pushed open the light blue door of the nurses' lounge. She poured a cup of coffee, flopped on the yellow vinyl couch with her legs stretched out on the seat, and picked up the *Chronicle.*

The next thing she knew, Mandie burst through the door, her face pale and drawn. She crumpled into a chair next to Kris and began to cry.

"Mandie, what in the world . . . What's wrong?" Tossing the paper aside, Kris bolted to her feet and threw her arms around her friend, stunned to feel Mandie's body shaking with silent sobs.

"Mandie . . . let me help!" she whispered.

Mandie sat up, sniffing and brushing at her tear-stained

cheeks with both hands. Her dark eyes, red and swollen, stared at Kris in unseeing despair.

"Oh, Kris. Dr. Gray just called." Her voice trembled and broke again. "The final tests are all back—the tissue has spread over the ovaries and fallopian tubes, and it's getting worse as I get older. Barring a miracle, Hank and I will never, ever have a baby!" She rushed through the words, her voice climbing until it broke.

"Oh, Mandie. There's no hope at all?" Kris felt as if her own heart would break.

"I suppose there's always hope . . . but my surgery four years ago and the new drug and all the tests add up to one thing: no baby. I feel as if the light in my life just went out." She pressed her lips together, struggling for control.

Kris covered Mandie's cold hand with hers. "Does Hank know yet?"

"No. I've got to get myself in hand before I tell him. Oh, Kris, we've been married over eight years. We've wanted a baby so much. I can't tell you how much. You know we both come from big families, and with Italian families like mine, babies are presumed! We haven't had the heart to tell Mom and Dad all we've been going through, so they have no idea. They've wallpapered and painted a room just for their grandchildren." She stared through the window at the ocean.

"Mandie, maybe this isn't the time to ask, but have you and Hank thought at all about alternatives? Maybe . . . adopting a baby?"

"We've talked about it a little. But we've always believed someday we'd have our own. It's hard to think of raising one that's not a part of Hank and me. We were so sure we'd eventually get pregnant." Her voice broke again.

"People adopt all the time. It takes work and planning and lots of support, but there's every sort of agency you could contact, when you feel ready. It might be worth a few phone calls."

They sat for a while in silence, Kris thoughtful, Mandie occasionally sniffing and blowing her nose as she fought waves of tears.

"In a way it's a relief to stop hoping," she said after several minutes, her voice low and edged with deep fatigue. "All those tests. It's gone on almost since Hank and I were married. One disappointment after another, one bill after another. I guess there's some consolation in finally facing reality. But poor Hank!" She clenched her fists, struggling not to cry again.

"Don't you think in a way he already suspects?"

"I'm sure he does. The subject of a baby's always with us, but we don't talk about it the way we used to. It hurts too much." Mandie reached for her purse, opened her compact, and groaned.

"I'll be a real inspiration on the floor . . . too bad it's not Halloween!" She managed a slight laugh and Kris hugged her shoulders, marveling at the way Mandie always seemed to pull up her wonderful sense of humor.

"I've got a bottle of lemon splash in my purse. Want to use it?"

"Thanks. I'll try anything." She walked to the mirror and dabbed the cool, lemony fragrance on her neck.

In her reflection Kris saw the sadness etched in Mandie's face, and winged a prayer to heaven. *Lord, You've told us if we lack wisdom to ask You for it. Well, I lack it, Lord. I really lack it, and so I'm asking.*

She looked out the window. "Mandie, would you like the rest of the day off? We're well staffed. You could go right away if you'd feel better."

"Thanks, but I'd be more depressed alone at home. Hank has a staff meeting after school, so he'll be late. I'd rather stay . . . if you don't think I'll scare the patients!" She tried to smile, handing back the bottle of splash.

Kris laughed. "You stay then. I agree you'd be better off busy. If Hank's working late, how about coming by my apartment after work? We could talk better there."

"I'd love it. Now I suppose we should get back to the floor."

Kris waited while Mandie dabbed at her makeup, awed by her friend's humility and courage.

LATE AFTERNOON SHADOWS almost covered the street as the two friends climbed the hill to Kris's apartment. Inside the sun beamed through the bay window, splashing over the luxuriant Boston fern.

"No wonder that thing's so healthy," Mandie said. "Looks like the sun's aiming straight for it." She tossed her yellow sweater on the wicker couch and stood in front of the fern. Though her face still looked drained, she seemed to be feeling more like herself. "Wish I could grow plants like you, Kris. What's your secret?"

"Oh, I fertilize them every week and mist the fern once in a while. And I order them to grow!" She laughed. "Tea or coffee? Or something else? I think I've got a Coke and a couple Seven-Ups."

Mandie followed her to the kitchen. "Oh, a cup of coffee, I guess. I could use some energy." She pulled out one of the kitchen chairs and rested her feet on the other.

"Mandie, how did it go today . . . overall, I mean? The afternoon got so busy I sort of lost track of you." Kris measured German chocolate grounds into her Braun coffee maker, a gift to herself last December. It had been her first Christmas away from home, and though she'd spent half the time at Hank and Mandie's, it hadn't been easy. The coffee maker helped.

"It was pretty hard until I got hold of Hank at lunchtime."

Chapter Seven

"How did he take it?"

"He amazed me. He wants a baby more than I do, if that's possible, but he was great. Tonight we're sending out for a pizza and having a long, long talk about this whole thing. I even mentioned what you said about adoption. We're going to take a hard look at that."

"Then it's a possibility?"

"Well, we need to explore the pros and cons a lot more. We've put it off, because we always thought we'd have our own baby. But now. . . ." Mandie stared out the window. "And even if we should decide to adopt," she finally continued, "that's no guarantee we'll be able to. Babies are hard to get, it can be expensive, and the wait can be years long. Besides, we're not getting any younger."

Kris put a plate of chocolate chip cookies on the table and poured the coffee into two white mugs. "Mandie, if adopting a baby is God's plan for you and Hank, nothing in all the world's going to stop that from happening. Remember, our God is in the miracle business!"

Mandie's eyes filled with tears as she cupped the hot mug between her hands. "Those words help more than you'll ever know."

Kris pointed to the wicker couch. "Right there's where I have my time with the Lord each morning. I'll be praying every single day for you and Hank to have that baby—one way or another!"

"Thanks, Kris." Mandie bit into a cookie. "These are great. Did you make 'em?"

Kris nodded. "I love to bake, but the problem is I also love to eat the results!"

"I know what you mean." A mischievous expression came over Mandie's face. "So, not to change the subject or anything, but how're things with you and Garth Endicott?"

"You never give up, do you? Well, he came over the other evening after work, and—"

"He what?" Mandie's feet hit the floor as she bolted upright in her chair. "He came over, and you didn't tell me?"

"Mandie, calm down! It wasn't what you think. There's nothing romantic about it."

"So what did he do? What did you talk about?"

"Well, we talked for a long time about how a person isn't ever alone when he knows Jesus. And Mandie, Garth's coming to church Sunday! I've been praying so hard for him. Doctors face such enormous problems, like little LeRoy Jones. There's no way they can handle it alone."

"That's great, Kris, that he said he'd come to church. Can we sit with you?"

"I was hoping you would. Garth got sort of serious when he was leaving, and I don't want him getting any unrealistic ideas."

Mandie's eyes narrowed. "Sort of serious? What happened the other night . . . exactly?"

"Oh, he thanked me for all we'd talked about. Our discussion really was beautiful. I think it meant a lot to him. And then he, well, he kissed my cheek."

"What? And you didn't tell me? Kris!" Mandie's voice was back to normal.

Kris couldn't help laughing. "Mandie, come on! It was only out of gratitude." She busied herself refilling their coffee mugs.

"Kris, my mug's almost full. Why are you pouring more coffee all of a sudden?"

Kris looked at her, embarrassed. "Oh, Mandie. Okay, it was more than gratitude. I admit it. But I still believe it's that he's really spiritually hungry. And when I see Todd tomorrow night, I'm going to tell him about all this, so he'll understand.

"Garth has some very hard things going on right now, and he needs answers. I'm suggesting the only answer that will last, and he's grateful. At least I think that's what it is. . . ."

Chapter Seven

Mandie searched her friend's face. "Kris, want to know what I think? I think he's falling in love with you."

A looming silence echoed through the sunny kitchen.

"Mandie, you're crazy. Maybe he's a little infatuated. But love? A man like that couldn't ever love someone like me."

"Kris, where do you get this stuff?"

"I'm from farming stock, Mandie. Grandma's right—we're simple people. When I was little, the doctor's children had their own friends. I didn't fit in with them then, and I don't now."

"Did it ever occur to you that you may be misjudging Garth? That he may not be what you've decided he is?"

"I'm positive. He'd be bored to death with me, if he didn't die of embarrassment first."

A call from Hank interrupted them.

"He's on his way to get me," Mandie reported. "Can you believe it's six o'clock already? Thanks—I really feel better!" She looked straight at Kris. "And I don't believe Garth's kiss had one thing to do with gratitude!"

Kris watched from the bay window until Hank's gleaming Chevy Nomad pulled away from the curb, then she flipped the TV dial to the evening news. But she heard little of it, as Mandie's parting words dominated her thoughts.

That night Kris prayed long for Garth. She poured out her confused feelings for him, praying that he would respond to the Holy Spirit's call on his life. But before she fell asleep, her unguarded mind drifted once again to the tender sweetness of his kiss.

8

WANT US TO GO IN and save some seats, Kris?" Mandie stepped away from the church's double doors as a bearded man with a crying toddler sidled through the animated crowd. His expectant wife followed, a bulging purse hanging from one shoulder and a red plaid diaper bag from the other.

The moment they left, Kris motioned Mandie and Hank back to the doorway. "Could you stay with me a few more minutes?"

Mandie pushed one hand deep into her green and white striped skirt pocket, exchanging a swift, knowing look with her husband. "We won't move an inch."

"I've never seen the gentleman in question," Hank announced, "but from what you ladies have told me, he may be coming now."

Kris stepped beyond the doors just as Garth arrived at the top of the stairs, and was stunned again by his casual good looks. His hazel eyes crinkled into a smile, their color intensified by a summer-weight tweed sport coat.

"Hi!" His voice was as warm as his eyes. "Hope I didn't

keep you waiting. Rounds took longer than usual."

"Perfect timing," she assured him. "Have you met Hank Dixon, Mandie's husband?"

"Good to meet you, Hank." Garth extended his hand. "I don't have to tell you that your wife is one fine nurse."

"Well, no, but it's good to hear, isn't it, Mandie?" Hank slipped an arm around his wife. "We'd probably better get into church. It's nearly eleven."

The four of them found seats halfway down on the left of the wide center aisle. Seated between Mandie and Garth, Kris adjusted the soft folds of her pink and beige print dress and tried to study the church bulletin . . . but the feel of Garth's rough coat against her arm and his unfamiliar nearness made concentration impossible.

As they stood for the opening hymn she was surprised to see nine high school and college-age students at the front of the church with Todd. They looked excited, and she wondered what sort of announcement they'd cooked up for today.

During the sermon Kris breathed a silent prayer of thanksgiving and praise for the pastor's message about worry. Surely the Lord had tailor-made it for Garth.

Halfway through, Garth pulled a Bible from the rack in front of them and thumbed through its pages.

"Where's Philippians?" he whispered.

Kris smiled, found the book he was looking for, and handed it back. His big hands turned to the fourth chapter one thin page at a time, and quickly located verses six and seven.

The pastor was summarizing his message in light of the Philippians passage.

"As someone joked," he said, "why pray when you can worry? But when we finally do quit worrying, a peace fills our lives unlike anything we've ever known." He leaned over the pulpit. "That kind of peace comes only from God, but it can belong to each one of us if we've trusted Jesus as Savior and Lord. Once we've made that decision, the Bible promises that His peace will keep our hearts at rest no matter what happens.

"Are you worried, or anxious, or can't get something off your mind? Or maybe looking to the world for answers it can never give? Why don't you quit struggling, and trust Jesus personally today? Why not give Him a chance? Tell Him about everything—every fear, every need, every inadequacy. And then leave it all in His hands, and watch Him work it out in ways you never dreamed."

Kris's eyes misted with tears as she marveled again at the mystery of God's perfect timing. Except for the day Danny Kee died, she'd never seen Garth's sensitive eyes more serious.

It seemed natural to bow their heads together as the minister led the congregation in a prayer of dedication or rededication of their lives to Christ. With all her heart Kris praised God for the miraculous way He had prepared Garth for this particular message.

As they finished the last verse of the closing hymn, Todd walked to the microphone. In just a few weeks, he told the congregation, he and the nine students with him would be leaving for a summer-long mission project in Zimbabwe, South Africa.

Kris looked up, stunned, struggling not to let her face reveal the shock she felt.

"It'll be a two-month undertaking," Todd continued, "and it won't be desk work for any of us. We'll do a little of everything: plumbing, school building construction, setting up community Bible studies.

"This has come up pretty fast, but it's a ministry we feel God has opened for us. The church is paying half of each student's costs, but we need more sponsors to turn the project into reality."

Chapter Eight

Todd stepped to the side of the pulpit. "If any of you feel this is a ministry you'd like to be part of, please see me after church. In the evening service we'll have a slide presentation that will give some specifics on the needs in Zimbabwe. The kids'll be ready to answer your questions, so be here if you can."

Kris felt betrayed. Only last night she and Todd had bought frozen yogurt cones after the youth group's softball game. Why hadn't he told her then he was leaving?

She thought back to their time on Fisherman's Wharf just a few weeks ago, how she'd turned away from his kiss. Maybe she hadn't been entirely fair to him, either. But to drop a bombshell like this in a Sunday morning service, without even a hint to her ahead of time. . . . She felt like a helium balloon cut from its moorings.

"Kris?" Garth asked as they worked their way up the crowded aisle. "If you don't have plans for this afternoon, I do. How about lunch, and then a drive down Lombard Street?"

His welcome invitation reeled in her wandering thoughts.

"I don't . . . and I'd love to. And believe it or not, I haven't been down Lombard Street yet. Everybody's heard of it or seen it in a movie, and it's embarrassing to admit I still haven't been there!" It would be good to stay busy, too busy to worry about whatever was going on with Todd.

As they neared the door Todd's eyes caught hers, and she imagined his smile seemed different, more guarded. But then she watched his hearty welcome for Garth, and changed her mind. His smile was the same as ever.

"Dr. Endicott, I'm Todd Franklin." He offered a hand with his distinctive brand of friendliness. "I saw you briefly at the Pavilion dedication."

"Todd . . . good to meet you. And the name's Garth. Enjoyed your comments up there. The work in Africa sounds impressive."

Garth spoke with conviction, and Kris enjoyed watching the exchange between these two very different men she cared about so much.

"The Lord's opened it up. There's no other way it could have happened. It'll be life-changing for the students—not to mention me!" Todd's blue eyes sparkled with enthusiasm. Then he looked at Kris.

"I owe you an apology, Kris. I would've told you about it sooner, but it all happened so fast. I've spent the past week on the phone."

Maybe, but that doesn't explain last night. "I . . . when is it you leave?"

"In early June. Haven't set the exact date. By the way, are you busy later? We could have lunch."

Her stomach turned over. "Oh, I'm sorry, Todd. I'm afraid I do have plans."

Todd smiled—a little too broadly, she thought. Something was different about him today. And whatever it was, having Garth along wasn't helping.

"Well, maybe tonight, then. Garth, good to have you here. Come back soon."

"Thanks, Todd. I appreciate that."

As they walked through the packed lobby, Kris fought off the impulse to rush back, to explain how worried Garth was about LeRoy, about the constant stress of being responsible for sick children, about how Garth had recently questioned her about her faith. She felt sure of only one thing—something was bothering Todd.

"There you are!" Mandie called from near the doors. "We've got to rush to a family picnic. Annual thing. And if we don't get there soon, the food will be gone!"

"Really good having you here," Hank said, shaking Garth's hand. "Hope you'll come back."

"I have a feeling I will. It means a lot being here. And thanks."

Chapter Eight

As the Dixons hurried into the bright noon sunshine, Garth rested a hand on Kris's shoulder.

"I've got it! Let's buy some French bread and salami and cheese and head up to Telegraph Hill. I know a picnic spot with a view of the city you won't believe."

His enthusiasm made her laugh. "It sounds great! But what about Lombard Street? Can we work that in?"

"Salami, bread, cheese, and Lombard Street, here we come!" Garth grabbed her hand and pulled her alongside him.

Kris laughed, feeling his energy as she raced with him down the stairs.

"Over there is Lombard Street. We'll drive down the crooked part when we leave."

Kris felt herself relax as Garth followed the winding road up Telegraph Hill. Changing patterns of lights and shadows danced over the Audi as they climbed. He had opened the sunroof and both windows, flooding the car with the perfumed scents of spring.

"This is it," Garth said after what seemed like only a few seconds. "The Telegraph Hill summit!"

Kris brushed her windblown hair back with both hands. The city stretched before them on every side, the view obscured only by the canopy of graceful trees arching above the parked car.

"What a view!" She stuck her head out the window and twisted it slightly, peering up at a squat, concrete structure. "That's Coit Tower, isn't it?"

"It is—all 210 feet of it. Built as a monument to the city's volunteer fire fighters. It's got a great view, but so does all of Telegraph Hill. Shall we scope out our picnic spot?"

Garth pulled off his tie and tossed it onto his sport coat

in the back seat. "Hungry?" he inquired with a smile, locking the car.

"As usual! I can't remember a day in my life when I wasn't hungry," Kris answered as he led her along a well-tended gravel path to the picnic area.

"And here it is, just waiting for us." He pointed to a small, unoccupied table at right angles to the path, half hidden by a large, pale pink rhododendron.

"This is the most incredible view I've ever seen," Kris sighed.

Below them the Presidio's buildings marched to the ocean like advancing geometric squadrons. The Golden Gate Bridge stood sentinel watch at the city entrance, gleaming gold and copper in the afternoon sun. Beyond stretched the deep blue waters of San Francisco Bay, edged by the probing, outstretched wharfs.

Despite its length of over four thousand feet, from their vantage point the bridge resembled a slender, glimmering thread gracefully spanning the water that separated the city of San Francisco from lush Marin County. To the east a second and longer bridge glowed like burnished silver. It arched to a small distant island, then jumped again to the far eastern shore.

Kris studied the magnificent view, absorbed by the city's indefinable beauty, and pointed to the closer bridge.

"That's the Bay Bridge, isn't it? From how it looks now, nobody would guess how damaged it was by the '89 earthquake. But what's the small island out there?"

"Treasure Island, where the 1939 World's Fair was held." Garth pointed straight ahead. "That's Yerba Buena Island right next to it. The Bay Bridge travels through a huge tunnel on Yerba Buena and ends in Oakland. It links San Francisco and the East Bay. Altogether it stretches about eight miles, one of the world's longest steel bridges. A smaller one goes from Yerba Buena to Treasure Island."

"The bridges are always so busy."

Garth nodded. "On Sunday afternoons they're especially full." He stood behind her, pointing over her shoulder. "Look right down there, Kris. San Francisco has twenty-four miles of waterfront. You can see all the wharfs, with Fisherman's Wharf over a little, more to the left. Have you been there yet?"

The memory of that windy, gray-blue afternoon flooded back. Though only a few weeks ago, it seemed an eternity since she had been there with Todd. He'd been so tender, so patient with her. "Yes . . . I've seen it."

"The memory's not all that good?"

She shook her head.

"Todd?"

Kris read the silent question in his eyes. "He's been a wonderful friend to me. He came to San Francisco about the same time I did. It'll be strange without him this summer."

"If I didn't know better, I'd say I'm not at all sorry he's going." Garth chuckled, breaking the conversation's serious turn. "You said you were starving a while ago. How about some lunch?"

"I'm ready!" Glad to change the subject, Kris brushed the rhododendron leaves from the picnic table with a paper napkin. "Oh, no! We forgot a knife."

"No, we didn't." Garth unhooked a pocket knife from his key chain. "Once a Boy Scout, always a Boy Scout!"

"I'm glad you had that," Kris said as he attacked the salami. "I always forget the essentials on picnics, like knives and bottle openers. Could I use it for the cheese?"

They admired the panoramic view as they ate. The distant hum of cars coming and going, the shrieks of children at play, the crunch of footsteps on gravel sounded from every section of the park. But the vivid rhododendron separating their table from the others gave them a pleasant sense of privacy.

The warm May breeze felt like velvet against her skin as Kris leaned her elbows on the table and watched the tiny distant sailboats racing on the Bay.

"Now I want to know," she said, pulling herself away from the view, "how did you feel about church this morning?"

It took him so long to answer she wondered if he'd heard her.

"I'll be up front," he finally said. "Somebody—I can't remember who—once said most men live lives of quiet desperation. I wouldn't say I've been desperate, but things have been piling up lately. Like LeRoy." He twirled a rhododendron leaf between his fingers.

"Using every medical approach we've got, he still has no guarantee of recovery. I shouldn't let it bother me so much, but it does." He snapped the leaf in two and tossed it to the ground. "So the minister's message and that part from the Bible really got to me."

"I'm glad, Garth."

"That's not all, Kris. You know that prayer after the sermon? Well, I prayed it along with him. I'm not sure if I'm good enough, or if God will have me. But whatever I am, this morning I . . . well, I gave it all to Him." He blinked several times and turned away.

Kris listened, her eyes luminous. She understood the step of faith Garth had taken, and her spirit soared with joy. Wherever his future led him, he would never again be alone.

"God knows all about those feelings. When we make up our minds to follow Him, He accepts us exactly where we are. It's a day-by-day adventure. A way of life."

"I sense that. I've seen it in you, Kris."

She smiled, embarrassed. "Do you have a Bible?"

"Somewhere. My grandmother gave me one when I was a kid. I'm afraid it's pretty dusty."

"That's easy to fix, but be sure to use one you can understand—there are lots of readable translations available. Have you thought about going to a Bible study?"

"Funny you should mention that. Ed McFarlane down in radiology invited me a couple of times to one that meets during lunch, but I've never gone."

"It's exactly what you need."

They sat for a while, listening to muffled footsteps as people came and went along the path. Finally Garth spoke, his voice tight with emotion.

"Kris, thanks. Thanks for caring enough to tell me about your faith and ask me to church."

"Following Jesus is the greatest adventure in life, Garth—I could never keep it to myself! And speaking of adventures, did I hear something earlier about Lombard Street?"

"Sure did. Let's clean up this stuff and we'll drive down Lombard on the way home."

In ten minutes they were there. Garth slowed the car at the top and Kris gasped. The tiny street, one block long, headed down the forty-degree slope in a breathtaking series of ten hairpin turns.

"Are you sure this is safe?"

"Positive. Been down it hundreds of times. Here we go!"

She clutched the edge of her seat as the car tipped forward. Kris was glad Garth drove slowly, and after two curves she relaxed enough to notice the homes on either side of them. Postage stamp lawns unfurled toward the street, ending against cement stairs that substituted for a sidewalk. Well-tended gardens flourished everywhere, and she was disappointed as the brief journey ended.

"Want to go down again?" Garth grinned.

"Oh, could we?"

"At your service. It's not called the crookedest street in the world for nothing!"

After three more trips down Lombard Street, the

deepening shadows hinted at the beautiful day's end. On the way back to Kris's apartment, Garth seemed unusually quiet.

She glanced at him several times, uneasy. All day he had been overflowing with energy and ideas.

"Garth, are you feeling all right? You're so quiet."

"I feel like a little kid on Christmas night," he told her, his voice strained. He pulled up to the curb and turned toward her, one hand on the steering wheel, the other on the back of the seat. "I don't want this day to be over."

She felt shaky, as though she were walking on ice about to crack open. "I know . . . but I guess even the best things have to end." Her hand curved over the door's handle. "And I'm afraid I do need to get—"

Her unfinished sentence hung in the air as Garth's powerful arms closed around her, pulling her against him. She drew back, but resistance vanished as his lips met hers. Her senses reeled with the nearness of him, the roughness of his skin, the gentle insistence of his kiss, his very scent. An unfamiliar wave of longing surged through her.

Then the blaring of a horn yanked her back to the present and she pulled away, breathless.

"I've wanted to hold you for so long, Kris. You're—"

Her thoughts tumbled one over another, a confusion of desire, panic, and an overpowering, desperate need to hide. Escape was her only hope.

"I-I've got to go. I'm sorry. The day was wonderful. I'll never forget it. But it's over now, and— I'll see you at work tomorrow."

Within seconds she was inside her apartment, blinded by the hurt and need in his eyes as she'd slammed the car door.

Tomorrow, she told herself from the safety of her darkened apartment. *Tomorrow he'll have more perspective. He'll remember who I am. A good nurse. A good friend who shared her faith with him. Period.*

Chapter Eight

Tears filled her eyes and she slumped onto the wicker couch, staring through the bay window at the dusky city. But hours later the powerful longing Garth's kiss had awakened still lingered, hovering like an emerging butterfly in the shadowed corners of her memory.

9

KRIS STARED THROUGH THE WINDOW at the leaden skies hovering over the city. Some day for a picnic. She grabbed her empty mug and stood up, wishing she could find a way to drive away the stifling fatigue she'd struggled against all week. Sound sleep had never been a problem, yet her rest had been fitful for days. Every time she closed her eyes she felt Garth's arms drawing her against him, saw the pain in his eyes as she pulled away.

Maybe she should call Mandie and Hank and bow out of the whole afternoon.

No, that wasn't right. Tired or not, she needed to be there. All three pediatric shifts looked forward to this annual event. She pulled her hair out from the neck of her old red sweatshirt, then drank a glass of water while she stared out the kitchen window.

Garth probably wouldn't come today, anyhow. Not after what had happened last Sunday. She'd been polite but withdrawn all week, certain he'd finally understood her message: the two of them were friends, nothing more. But if that were so right, whispered a nagging voice, why did she still feel so miserable?

At least there were plenty of women around to comfort him—cultured, sophisticated women who would know exactly how to pick up the pieces of his wounded ego. And at the head of the line would march Sybil Trefts.

Just get out of the way, Kris told herself, *before anybody else gets hurt. Things will take care of themselves.*

She checked her watch for the third time in fifteen minutes and poured herself a fresh cup of coffee. Hank and Mandie would be there in another hour—maybe she should do something productive before they arrived.

Immediately she dismissed the thought and sat down at the kitchen table. The geranium's blooms were gone now, and though the foliage was green and glossy, she missed its brilliant crimson flowers. Better pick up some fish fertilizer tomorrow after church.

Church. Todd. She hadn't seen him all week, he was so busy getting ready for Zimbabwe. She stirred her coffee, watching the spoon create small dark whirlpools.

She smiled. How alike they were in so many ways. His single-minded pursuit of the mission trip seemed like a carbon copy of her own preparation for nursing and graduate school. Nothing else got in the way.

Grandma would approve of Todd. "He's our kind of people," she would say. Uncomplicated, hard-working. No pretense. No fear of embarrassing him with what she didn't know, because he wouldn't know, either. A life with Todd would be safe and secure.

The phone rang and she jumped. With a practiced reach Kris searched out the receiver without turning around.

"Hello?"

The only answer was a strange, slow breathing.

"Hello. Who is it ?"

"Missing . . . but not lost . . ." breathed a sibilant voice.

She listened, motionless, certain she had heard the voice before. What did the words mean?

She slammed down the receiver, wondering when children's phone games had become so frightening.

Almost immediately the phone rang again. On the twelfth ring she reluctantly picked it up.

"Hello?"

"Just wanted to let you know we'll be there about twelve-thirty," Mandie bubbled. "Okeydoke?"

Kris relaxed all over. "I'll be ready," she promised. "Uh, Mandie . . . did you call a minute ago?"

"No."

"Well, somebody did. Probably kids playing tricks." She shuddered as her mind replayed the short, hissing words. "Wish the sun would come out."

"Weatherman said it would clear up later on. Hope you will, too—you sound like a cloud about to rain!"

"This hasn't been one of my favorite weeks . . ."

"I don't think I've ever seen you so down. Kris, you haven't told me what happened last Sunday. Garth's been acting strange, too. Is he coming today?"

"I doubt it. I made it pretty clear how I feel. Or rather, how I don't feel. I'll be surprised if he shows up." She tried to sound convincing.

"You just might be. Is your salad ready?"

"Fixed it night before last. I made that big pasta and olive one that needs to marinate a day or two."

"I love pasta in any form! Now cheer up. It's going to be a great afternoon. We'll be over in less than an hour."

Kris hung up feeling better. Mandie had a special way of making her laugh, and today she needed that gift. She stretched, then pushed a tape into the stereo. She needed something to get her moving.

Chapter Nine

"Hank, help! We can't carry another thing," Mandie wailed. "What'll we do about the salads?" She shifted a stack of bulky beach towels to her left arm, trying to get a better grip on the portable radio.

"Unless we want them flavored with leaves and bark dust, I suggest we leave 'em here," Hank answered, balancing four folding chairs on his shoulders. "They're on ice, aren't they?"

"More or less. They'll probably be all right for a couple of hours. What do you think, Kris?"

"I vote to leave 'em in the car. We can come back when they're ready to serve."

As they neared the picnic area the babble of voices helped Kris realize she wouldn't have missed this for anything. Thanks to the Pavilion's low census at the moment, almost everyone had been able to come.

Rimmed by enormous green trees, the entire children's playground of Golden Gate Park had been reserved for the MacKenzie Pavilion staff.

"Mandie! Kris!" Ruby Cates, her yellow and red Hawaiian shirt impossible to miss, met them on the bark-strewn path.

Kris could only guess at the effort Ruby had poured into this year's event. Clever signs hung from a rope circling several tree trunks, each describing with arrows and cartoon stick-people the location of the many available activities. A cluster of balloons decorated each sign, brightening the overcast day. Red, white, and blue paper cloths covered every table, already groaning with the steadily arriving food. Animated conversation mingled with music from one end of the picnic area to the other.

"This is wonderful, Ruby. You've done a fantastic job!"

"Isn't she something else?" Carmen Martinez hugged Ruby's shoulders. "Hate to admit it, but I think this is the best ever!"

Before Kris could answer, Garth appeared carrying two bulging grocery sacks. His eyes brushed hers and looked away. All week she'd hoped he wouldn't come, but there he was. She muttered something to Ruby and Carmen and moved around the tables toward him. At least she could try to patch up the embarrassing gulf between them.

"Hi, Kris." He pulled bags of potato chips from a sack, his face tense.

"Hi. Garth, I . . . I'm sorry things have been so awkward."

He looked straight at her, bewilderment still mirrored in his eyes. "Kris, I just wish we could talk. What time is dinner?"

"Not for a couple hours."

"How about renting some bikes? The park's a good three miles long, with great trails."

"Thanks, but I don't think so." She groped for an acceptable excuse. "I told Ruby I'd help set up."

"They've got more help than they know what to do with. Come on, Kris. I promise not to bite." A subtle challenge edged his voice.

Maybe he was right. And after all, friends could ride bikes together. She tightened the white elastic band around her hair. "All right. I'll tell Mandie and Hank where I'm going."

Ten minutes later they were pedaling over a well-paved bike path edged by immaculate, bark-covered beds carpeted with yellow and bronze marigolds. They rode single file, Garth in the lead, the muscles of his upper arms and back clearly visible through the loose weave of a yellow knit shirt that tapered to his narrow hips. He seemed more at ease now, glancing back often to flash her a reassuring smile.

The sound of music drifted toward them, and Garth signaled her to pull over.

Chapter Nine

"Hear that? It's from the outdoor stage—Handel's 'Music for the Royal Fireworks.' Golden Gate Park has concerts almost all year long." He smiled down at her, pushing his hair back with his fingers.

"I like it. I wish I knew more about that kind of music." She thought about the small wooden radio Grandma kept on the back porch. At six every night they used to listen to the farm report, but most of the time the radio was turned off. Grandma said too much music weakened your brain.

"Want to sit down and listen for a few minutes?"

They found a bench near the concert area and parked their bikes beside them. Kris tipped her face to the sun's warmth, pleased that it was burning off the morning fog.

"Kris, I guess I was out of bounds last weekend," Garth apologized. "I'm sorry. But I want you to know I went to Ed's Bible study. About ten of the medical staff were there—I was surprised. I'm planning to go again." His eyes, clear and direct, appealed for understanding.

"I'm so glad, Garth. And don't apologize. I was pretty rude."

Kris was aware of the curve of his tanned forearm on the bench behind her. She longed for their uncomplicated professional status of only a few months ago, when everything had been so much simpler. When had the doctor become a man, and the nurse a woman?

She felt his hand touch hers.

"Friends?" he said with a smile.

She smiled back, noticing something warm yet guarded in his hazel eyes . . . something she couldn't identify and hadn't seen before. Then he stood, pointing to the bikes.

"How about it? Ready for more?"

Kris laughed, relieved. "Ready!" It was good to move on, leaving the awkwardness behind them.

The rest of the ride sped by in a blur of swirling clouds and slender shafts of sunlight. Flowers, brooding trees, tourists, and children were everywhere. The ride seemed to end before it began.

"This park is incredible," she said, catching her breath as they pulled up to the rental store an hour and a half later.

"And we've only scratched the surface. Maybe we can come back someday when we have more time, and see more of what's here. There's a Japanese tea garden, museums, a planetarium, lakes."

"I'd love to explore more of it," Kris acknowledged as they walked back to the picnic area.

"Hi, you two!" Mandie called. "How was the ride?"

"Beautiful! I had no idea this park was so large," Kris answered as Garth greeted Hank.

"I grew up playing hide-and-seek in it," Mandie laughed. "We still have our family picnics here each summer. Speaking of picnics, they're getting dinner underway. We could put out our salads any time now."

"Why don't you give me the keys, and I'll go get them?"

"Okay, if you're sure you can carry both."

Deep contentment rippled over Kris as she retraced the path to Hank and Mandie's car and lifted her face to the still-cool afternoon breeze. The invigorating bike ride had dispelled her long week's fatigue and discouragement. What a relief it was to have things straightened out with Garth. His friendship meant a lot, she told herself, and she hoped it would continue.

She spotted the Dixons' distinctive Chevy Nomad beyond a light green van and walked faster, eager to rejoin the party.

"At last, Miss Carothers. I've been waiting for you."

She stopped, frightened. Only a second ago the parking lot had looked empty, except for cars. She took a step back, her heart pounding as a man wearing shorts and Birkenstock sandals emerged from the shadows. Dr. Burack.

Chapter Nine

"Did . . . did you come to the picnic?" Kris stammered, certain he could hear the drumbeat of her heart.

"I choose not to take part in most things at University Hospital, Miss Carothers." He stared over her head, avoiding her eyes. "But I thought I'd drop by this particular event because I have something that may interest you."

"Me?"

"Yes." He placed one hand over the other and stretched them towards her, then lifted the upper hand. Across his palm lay her missing scissors.

Kris shuddered, feeling stripped and helpless before him. "How . . . where did you find them?"

"Never mind, Miss Carothers. I know many things about you. Many things. But you are much too busy for me," he continued. "Perhaps so beautiful a woman has too many men in her life. But if you knew what I could—"

"Kris!" Mandie's voice, soaring from the edge of the parking lot, had never sounded so good.

"Mandie, over here!" Kris yelled back with all her strength.

"What's taking you so long?" Mandie called, running down the path. "Oh, Dr. Burack!" She stopped short.

"Mrs. Dixon, how very nice to see you. I was just returning something to Miss Carothers. If you'll excuse me. . . ." He walked ten feet to a sleek blue Cadillac and a moment later sped away.

"Kris, you're pale. Whatever was that man doing here?"

Shivering, Kris threw her arms around Mandie. "I'm so glad you came when you did! I think he was waiting out here, hoping I'd show up alone. I have no idea how he got hold of my missing scissors. The only thing I'm sure of is that I never want to see him again!"

"He's weird all right, but I can't believe he meant any harm." Mandie opened the car door. "Has he ever actually done anything?"

"Not really. It's what he says."

"Well, it wouldn't hurt to avoid him as much as possible."

"I do, Mandie. But I've got the strangest feeling that he watches me. He knows too much about what I'm doing." Kris held both salads while Mandie locked the car.

"I'm sure you're imagining it. But let's see what Hank and Garth think, all the same."

Dense smoke from the sizzling hamburgers hung suspended over the lively crowd. Kris and Mandie found Hank and Garth hoisting the last of four freezers of homemade ice cream to the dessert table.

"You two look awfully serious," Hank said. "Something wrong?"

Kris looked at the two men, wondering where to begin. "I just went to the parking lot to get our salads, and—" Her voice trembled. "Dr. Burack was out there, alone, as though he'd been watching for me."

"That guy never comes to any social events. What did he want?" Garth demanded.

"He had my scissors. My engraved ones that I've been missing for weeks. But the way he gave them back was so strange." Kris shook her head. "He could have given them to me at work any day."

"He came clear out here to give you back a pair of scissors?" Hank asked.

"That's what he said. He also went on about how I'm always too busy for him."

"I'd give the man a wide berth, Kris," Garth cautioned. "I'm sure he's harmless, but steer clear of him all the same."

"I try to! But I feel as if he always knows where I'm going, what I'm doing."

"I think some food would do us all good." Hank pointed to the barbecue. "Anybody else ready for dinner?"

It felt good to be surrounded by friends in the

hamburger line. With full plates they joined the rest of the staff around the large bonfire pit.

The memory of Fred Burack's staring eyes dimmed as Kris polished off a hamburger, salads, chips, and homemade ice cream.

"Oh give me land, lots of land, under starry skies above," someone sang out. Soon other voices joined in. Kris crossed her arms and leaned forward, spellbound by the music and the bonfire's glowing embers.

"Cold?" Garth asked.

"A little. Forgot my sweater."

Without a word he pulled off his brown khaki jacket and slipped it over her shoulders. She smiled at him and snuggled into its reassuring warmth.

10

THE PAVILION HAD BEEN A MADHOUSE since the moment Kris arrived. Admissions, endless phone calls, incessant questions. If only someone would figure out how to eliminate Mondays.

But Jesus promised to be with me in everything, she reminded herself. *Even on Monday mornings.*

Carmen answered the phone and handed it to Kris. "It's Phyllis down in ER She's got another one for us."

Kris took the phone.

"We're bringing a patient up in about five minutes. Accidental poisoning."

"Any details?"

"Fifteen-month-old girl. Found her mom's sleeping pills on the bedside table and swallowed about half."

"How far have you gone with her?"

"She's too drowsy for Ipecac, so we pumped her stomach. She'll be an overnight."

"Okay. We'll be looking for you. Thanks." The moment she hung up, the phone rang again.

Chapter Ten

Kris covered the receiver with one hand. "Carmen, could you let Mandie know? I've got her down with the little ones today. She'll need to set up."

"MacKenzie Pavilion," she answered. "Miss Carothers speaking."

"Good, it's you, Kris. This is Susan Phillips. Can you hold for a minute? Mr. Talbot wants to talk to you."

Before Kris had time to wonder what the hospital administrator wanted, the elevator snapped open and Nineveh two-stepped to the nurses' station. He plopped down a large stack of mail on the counter, made two waving circles at her, and left.

"Kris? Ron Talbot. Sorry to keep you waiting."

"I was glad to sit still a minute, Mr. Talbot. We're having a typical Monday morning."

"I'm afraid my news may not help. We had a call this morning from an organization called Operation Search. Have you heard of it?"

"They've spoken at our church. As I remember, they seek out underprivileged children in need of specialized medical care. They're all over the world, aren't they?"

"That's the one. I've been on the phone with them most of the morning. Several weeks ago they learned about a Korean baby in need of heart surgery. Little girl. Escorts for her turned up several weeks sooner than they'd expected, and an airline donated travel space."

"She's coming here for the surgery?"

"Yes. She'll probably arrive late this morning."

"Do we know any details? What about her family?'

"Apparently she's been in an orphanage all her life, but they're doing what they can to locate the natural parents. I've been concentrating on getting her here. She's coming on a visitor's visa for emergency care."

"And she's arriving this morning?"

Carmen, listening to Kris's side of the conversation,

rolled her eyes as she flipped open a new chart.

"Late, but yes," answered Mr. Talbot. "The diagnosis has been prescreened, so she'll be a candidate for surgery. I know how many admissions you've already had today, Kris, but University was the organization's first choice, because of our facilities and surgical team."

"Mr. Talbot, I think it's exciting. Operation Search has helped more children around the world than any group I know of. If we can have a part in that, it's worth it."

"Keep saying it, Kris! I'll be in touch as I learn more."

Kris hung up the phone as Mandie arrived and leaned over the nurses' station counter.

"Your face is a dead giveaway, Kris. What's going on?"

"Mr. Talbot just called. You've got another one coming into your unit today. A Korean baby. Probable heart surgery."

"I'll have a set-up prepared. Any information about her?"

"Not yet, but we should soon. She'll probably arrive late this morning. Coming straight from the airport."

"I'll get right on it." Mandie looked toward the elevator. "Looks like the baby from the ER's here."

An emergency room orderly pulled a small crib over the elevator threshold as Phyllis steadied a swaying bottle of intravenous fluid.

"Hi, Phyllis," Mandie called, falling in step beside the other nurse. "Bring her right this way. How's she doing?"

"Pretty rough time of it, but after she sleeps it off she'll be fine."

The fast-moving trio rolled down the hall, trailed by a young woman in a red jersey jump suit. Inside the crib's chrome bars their pint-sized patient slept soundly, unaware of her almost-fatal venture.

"Kris, guess what's in today's mail," Carmen said.

"Another patient?"

"Well, sort of. It's from a former patient."

Chapter Ten

"Who?" Kris demanded, momentarily ignoring the mountain of work facing her.

"Tommy Monroe!" Carmen announced, handing a small sheet of paper to Kris. "He wrote us a letter!"

Kris skimmed the smudged, ten-line treasure, her eyes shining.

"Sounds like he's having the time of his life at diabetic camp! Horseback riding, archery—and he's learning about food exchanges and how to inject his own insulin. He'll have so much more confidence from this!" She handed the letter back to Carmen. "Let's leave it on the counter for the other shifts. Later on we'll stick it on the bulletin board."

Kris grabbed a clipboard, patting her pocket to be sure she still had a pen. "I'll be in Dr. Endicott's office for a few minutes. Need orders for Operation Search's baby."

On her way down the hall she dodged a wagon propelled by a grinning, dark-skinned boy. Though a cast covered one leg from ankle to hip, his ability to break the Pavilion speed limit was unimpaired.

"Slow it down, Brad," Kris warned, "or you won't get to play with the Nintendo tonight." Before the sentence was out of her mouth, the wagon skidded to a stop.

At the utility room door she stood to one side while a large chrome work cart emerged, loaded to capacity with mops, pails, plastic bags, and huge stock bottles of liquid soap and Betadine. She smiled down at the short gray-haired woman guiding it into the hall.

"There you are, Sophie. I couldn't see you behind all those supplies."

"Morning, Miss Carothers! Glad you came by. I've done some more embroidery," she said, looking down. "You could see it later, if you have time." Her bright eyes were warm and friendly, two blue islands in a pink and white face devoid of makeup. At the back of her stout neck a thick gray braid coiled to a neat bun.

"For your church, Sophie?"

"Yes. Altar cloths." The soft voice vibrated with pride.

For years Kris had admired the exquisite needlework of this first-generation Greek woman. "I want to see them for sure. I'll be by sometime this afternoon!" She smiled down at her friend before hurrying on.

Ten feet up the hall she spotted Garth lounging in his office doorway, deep in conversation with LeRoy Jones. From the pillowed comfort of a large red wagon, extended at its sides by wooden slats, the little boy looked up at the world around him. His mother stood nearby, one hand on the wagon's handle, obviously enjoying the friendship between her son and his doctor. Since LeRoy had gotten sick she'd slept every night on a narrow bed in his room.

"Hi, Miss Carothers!" LeRoy's pale face broke into a wide grin.

"Hi, yourself! You're managing to get around pretty well in that thing, aren't you?" Kris smiled back, concerned that LeRoy had lost even more of his dark hair in the last day or two. On the pillow beside him rested Ratty Raccoon, the top of his stuffed head shaved close to match LeRoy's baldness.

"Come on, son," his mother urged. "We've taken up enough of the doctor's time." She eased LeRoy back on the pillows and pulled the wagon forward.

"Bye, LeRoy," Garth called. "See you this afternoon."

Kris moved her clipboard to the other hand. "Talk to you for a minute?"

"Of course, come on in." Garth motioned to an empty chair and sat down at his desk. "LeRoy stops by several times a day. He's quite a guy."

"He seems a little better the last three days. How do you think he's doing, overall?"

"He's responding well to the treatment protocol. Radiation and chemotherapy are taking a toll, of course, but he'll bounce back from that. Ninety-three percent of children treated for Hodgkin's never have a relapse. His prognosis is excellent."

"That's wonderful." She leaned back, smiling. "I have some other good news. We got a letter from Tommy Monroe. He's at diabetic camp and loving it."

Garth made a drumbeat on his desk blotter with a Bic pen. "That's the kind of news that makes my day."

"On a different subject, I'm here because we have a Korean baby due in this afternoon. Operation Search learned about her through missionaries in Korea. She's been prescreened, and they're all but sure she has a heart defect. No other information at this point, but I wondered what kind of preliminary orders you'd like."

Garth said nothing for a moment. "Let's put her in the four-crib room for starters. Regular diet. Electrocardiogram. Complete blood work-up. And you could go ahead and tentatively schedule a cardiac cath for her, Kris. We'll do a complete diagnostic work-up, but if there's a heart problem, she'll need catheterization. Parents?"

"They're not sure She's been living in an orphanage."

"Age?"

"Not sure of that, either," Kris laughed. "But I'd guess under twelve months."

"Not sure of what?"

In the doorway stood Sybil Trefts, poised and radiant in a turquoise blue crepe de chine dress and matching Ferragamo sling pumps.

"Sybil, good to see you." Garth stood, reaching for an extra chair. "Please, sit down."

Sybil's lips curled into a demure, little-girl smile as she entered the room. Her ultra sheer nylons whispered an expensive message as she slowly crossed one shapely leg over the other. Kris couldn't help admiring the copper highlights in her hair, dazzling even under the office's fluorescent light.

"I'm glad to find you both in one place," Sybil said, her voice purring like a well-tuned motor. "The auxiliary's fall fund-raiser is moving ahead nicely. But before we go any further, we must run over some details, Garth." She looked to one side, fluttering her eyelids. "And Kris."

Feeling like a wooden puppet with a painted smile, Kris acknowledged the token words. How could anyone look that good on Monday morning?

The flat, serviceable nursing shoes that carried her through eight-and ten-hour days suddenly looked oversized and ugly. Even her natural fingernails seemed pale and ordinary compared to Sybil's, long, curved, and lustrous with dark beige polish. The contrast was inescapable.

Stop it, she told herself. *You and Sybil work together, not against each other.* She looked up, determined to at least try and act interested.

"What kind of fund-raiser is it?"

One finely shaped eyebrow twitched as silence hung in the room like an embarrassing odor.

"There's only one kind of fund-raiser, dear. One that makes money, and lots of it!" Her singsong words made it sound as if she were addressing a child.

Garth cleared his throat as Kris's hands grew cold. "How do you plan to do that, Sybil?"

Sybil leaned back with a tolerant chuckle. "Well, dear, you and I know there's only one way these things should be done—with a luncheon at the best hotel in town. Style show from I. Magnin's. Exciting speakers. A huge silent auction." She gave a slight shrug. "The sort of thing we've grown up doing." Turning her back on Kris, she focused her gaze on Garth. "Remember the money-raising adventures for our senior ball?"

Kris's face flushed with anger.

Garth looked uncomfortable, shifted in his chair, and again cleared his throat.

Chapter Ten

"So, Sybil . . . where does pediatrics fit in with all this?"

"Two ways." She leaned toward him, pad and pencil in hand, deliberately sensual. "First, the committee simply can't imagine anyone but you as our featured speaker, Garth. Would you consider it? And second, what are the Pavilion's most urgent requirements?"

She'd pushed the magic button, and with every word Garth's enthusiasm grew.

"First question's easy," he replied. "I'd be happy to. And the second's easy, too. We need another portable monitor. In fact, we could use two. And if any money's left over, we'd still like to put in carpeting and some sort of mural in the—"

"Hold it!" Sybil laughed, tossing her hair in the now-familiar way. "I've made note of all your needs, and I promise to give them everything I've got!"

Kris gripped the clipboard and stood up. "Excuse me. I must get back. I'm sure the two of you have everything under control."

Garth bumped into Sybil's chair as he rushed to the door. "I'll be down later to write orders for the new admissions, Kris. And thanks—" He looked as though he wanted to say something else, but changed his mind.

Kris hurried away, grateful for the cool, wide hall. It was good to be back in her own world, good to hear the busy morning sounds of the Pavilion. Sybil and Garth's fancy affairs and fund-raisers weren't for her. She wanted no part of them. But there was no doubt in her mind about one thing. Before very long Sybil Trefts would become Mrs. Garth Endicott . . . or die trying.

Kris rounded the corner to the nurses' station as the elevator doors opened for the hospital administrator and two women, each carrying a large shoulder purse and shopping bag. One cradled a small baby.

"There you are, Kris," Carmen said, replacing the intercom phone. "Tried to catch you in Dr. Endicott's office. The patient from Operation Search just arrived." She nodded at the elevator. "Got an earlier flight than expected."

"Thanks, Carmen. Would you notify Mandie and Dr. Endicott that they're here?" She walked over to greet the small party.

"Miss Carothers," Mr. Talbot said warmly, "our baby arrived sooner than we'd thought. But not soon enough for her escorts, I suspect, who've been up all night. I'd like you to meet Katherine Wright and Vicki Sanchez."

Kris shook hands with the two women, whose eyes were rimmed with dark circles.

"Welcome to University Hospital, both of you. And welcome to your little friend!"

With a practiced eye she studied the baby sleeping in Mrs. Sanchez's arms. As almost always with these cases, the infant was too sleepy and small for her age, and much too quiet. Kris gestured down the hall.

"Why don't you all come with me, and we'll get her settled?"

She led them to a sunny room with four cribs. All but one held a young patient, including the deeply sleeping baby recently arrived from emergency, a Ratty Raccoon propped in a far corner of her crib.

Mandie met them at the door, smiled as Kris introduced her, and walked to the one vacant crib.

"You can put her down right here. And her name?"

"Kyung," Miss Wright volunteered. "Kyung Lee." She spelled both words. "She's twelve months old."

Startled, Kris looked at the baby again. She looked more like four months, or even younger. No matter how many heart defects she saw, these children's abnormal growth patterns always shocked her.

Kyung opened her jet-black eyes as Mrs. Sanchez gently lowered her to the bed. Despite the unfamiliar surroundings, she showed little interest and no apparent fear. A subtle bluish color tinged her tiny mouth and the tips of her nose, fingers, and toes, mute evidence of her defective heart.

After a brief physical assessment Mandie visited with the baby's escorts, trying to dig out anything else they knew about her.

Kris bent over the crib. "Hello, Kyung," she whispered. The almost-round, unblinking black eyes stared up at her. She looked like a tiny, olive-skinned doll of fragile beauty. How wonderful to think that if the pre-diagnosis were right, one operation could restore her to health.

"Did either of you meet Kyung's parents?" Mandie was asking.

Mrs. Sanchez shook her head. "As far as we know, she was abandoned right after birth. Someone left her in the train station during the night, on a bench where she'd be sure to be found."

"The police sent her to an orphanage right away," Miss Wright added. "Been there ever since. She's Korean-American, so doesn't stand much chance of acceptance by her own people. She'll probably grow up in the orphanage."

Mandie nodded and scribbled notes.

Kris stood behind her, listening as she studied the lethargic baby. Her home was an orphanage. She'd been rejected by her own people, doubtless rarely stimulated or held. Small wonder she was so underdeveloped, so unresponsive. And her heart defect alone would explain her obvious fatigue and failure to thrive.

Mandie looked puzzled. "How did the two of you come to escort her over?"

"We're elementary school teachers, just finishing a trip through Korea and the Far East," Mrs. Sanchez answered. "Both of us are supporters of Operation Search, so before we left we let them know we were available if they needed us." She smiled, deep fatigue lines crinkling around her eyes. "We never imagined they'd use us, but it's something we both wanted to do."

"You probably saved this baby's life," Kris said quietly. "The surgery she needs isn't available in her country. And every day without it means she loses ground."

"The real hero is Operation Search," Miss Wright added. "They knew about her, and when an opening came they wouldn't give up."

The women left to get some sleep at a nearby motel, promising to call in twenty-four hours about Kyung's progress.

Kris glanced at the chrome-rimmed clock above her desk and recalled her brittle encounter with Sybil Trefts only an hour before. Sybil had been openly hostile, obviously not caring who saw it. Ignoring her insult was hard, but Kris was glad she had.

Picturing Garth and Sybil together was more than a little difficult . . . but sooner or later a person could get used to almost anything. She opened Kyung's new chart, grateful that God had called her into nursing, caring for His little ones.

LATE THAT AFTERNOON, Kris and Mandie walked to a table in the almost-empty Roof Restaurant.

"What a day." Kris pulled a chair out and sat down heavily, closing her eyes.

"How many admissions, all together?" Mandie asked.

"Fourteen, I think. I lost count."

"My feet tell me you're right on target," Mandie said with a laugh. "Hank's coming by soon. At four-thirty we've got an appointment with an adoption agency. Can we drop you by your apartment?"

"I'd love it. Not sure I could walk three whole blocks." She leaned back, yawning. "The picnic was great, wasn't it?"

CHAPTER TEN

"I don't know when I've had more fun. Or better food!"

Kris nodded, remembering the staff's blended voices as twilight settled over the park. For a day that had begun so dismally, Saturday had turned into a welcome surprise. Everything about it had been wonderful, especially mending her friendship with Garth. The only bad part had been Dr. Burack's strange appearance, but at least she hadn't seen him since.

"Before I leave, I want to stop by and see Sophie," Kris added. "It'll just take five minutes."

"You and Sophie," Mandie teased. "Has she been doing more handwork?"

"Yes. She's truly an artist with the needle. I wish I—" Kris stopped, her face frozen.

"What's wrong?"

Directly across the room Dr. Burack had just sat down. He stirred the ice in his glass, his face impassive, staring at the wall beyond Kris.

"Mandie, I'm sorry," Kris whispered. "Can we leave? Dr. Burack's over there. The man gives me the creeps."

As one they stood together, their backs towards him.

"Bring your coffee," Kris said. "We can go to the nurses' lounge."

But even there his melancholy face dominated her mind, despite Mandie's reassurance. Right after their break she'd find Garth and review orders—something they needed to do anyhow. Somehow he always made her feel safe.

"You two back already?" Carmen called. "Thought you just left!"

"We decided to have our coffee down here," Kris explained. "By the way, Carmen, when you see Dr. Endicott, would you tell him I'd like to run over patient orders in a few minutes?"

"Dr. Endicott? He said he'd be back tonight, after dinner. He just left. He and Miss Trefts."

11

KRIS RACED UP THE STAIRS and across the church lobby, adjusting her beige canvas purse as she smoothed her hair. The warm, lengthening days of early June had lightened it to the color of ripe flax, the humidity making it harder than ever to control. In a rush to get to the Wednesday evening service, she'd tied it back with a blue ribbon, hoping to feel cooler in the unexpected San Francisco heat wave. She pulled open the sanctuary door and found an empty pew near the back.

This informal midweek service with its graded, planned activities for all the family was her favorite. Many members of the congregation referred to it simply as family night. A good description.

"Penny for your thoughts!"

"Hi," she whispered, surprised to see Todd sit down beside her. Announcements were under way, and the short service would soon begin. "I've hardly seen you lately. You must be swamped getting ready to go."

He nodded. "It's probably a good thing I didn't know what

was involved in a project like this, or I might have changed my mind! What with planning for passports, money, correspondence, programs, shots . . . it's been incredible."

"You leave pretty soon, don't you?"

"Early Monday. I'd like to see you before then, Kris. Maybe for dinner?"

"That would be nice. How's Friday night?"

"Great. Can I pick you up about five-thirty, or is that too early?"

It did seem early, but his schedule had been crammed to overflowing since the mission to Zimbabwe began. "No, of course not. I'll be ready."

"Good. I need to get down front. See you later." He squeezed her hand and hurried to the front of the church as the congregation stood to sing.

Kris watched him—muscular, trim, controlled. It would be good to have some time alone together before he left. He needed to know about her feelings for him since their windy day at Fisherman's Wharf. And she needed to be sure he understood exactly why Garth had been with her so much lately.

An overhead projector beamed a praise song onto the screen down in front. "You shine, like the morning star. Jesus, what a wonder You are."

Kris looked away, trying to memorize the words. Wednesday night's songs were newer, less familiar than Sunday's. They were simple hymns, often taken directly from Scripture, hymns she loved to recall during long hours of work.

As they began the last stanza Kris again looked away to test her memory—and saw Garth walking down the aisle. Immediately she forgot every word. A midweek service was the last place she'd expected to see him.

As he slipped into the pew beside her, she felt her face flush a deep red. Furious at herself, she turned away. Why did she get these silly attacks of blushing whenever something unexpected happened? It had nothing to do with Garth. Still, she felt ridiculous and was glad when the song ended and she could sit down.

"Hi," he whispered, leaning toward her. "Hope you weren't saving this seat."

He didn't seem to have noticed the color of her face.

"No. It's good to see you here."

She was delighted to see Garth open his own Bible as the pastor began the lesson. He located the passage announced and took an active part in the discussion as the class progressed.

Kris listened, amazed at his unmistakable spiritual growth. Somebody in the front row asked a question, and during the pastor's involved answer Kris looked at Garth, her blue-gray eyes sparkling.

"Is that the Bible your grandmother gave you?" she whispered. "The one that used to be a little dusty?"

Garth smoothed its well-marked page with his hand. "No, this is a newer translation, with the kind of language we use. And it's never been dusty yet." He looked at her. "But I do have some questions. Do you have any time after the service?"

Todd was looking their way, and Kris lowered her voice even more. "I'll be glad to give it a try."

"We could pick up some ice cream," he whispered.

Kris smiled. "With this heat, that sounds wonderful. We could take it to my apartment." How natural it felt to invite him there—so different from only a few weeks ago. "The service won't go later than seven-thirty because of the children."

During the final twenty minutes she tried hard to pay attention to the lesson. But Todd kept looking in her direction, making it impossible to concentrate. It was a relief when the service ended and she and Garth walked into the lobby. As he headed for the door, she touched his arm.

Chapter Eleven

"Let's say hi to Todd."

"Sure, I'd like to see him."

The broad smile on Todd's face as he neared them lightened her heart. If he did have any misconceptions about her friendship with Garth, he certainly hid it well.

"Hi, Garth!" he said, extending his hand. "Great to see you. Hope you enjoyed the service."

"Very much. I've wanted to come before, but so far something always seems to happen on Wednesday nights."

"I know how that goes! I've got to get downstairs—the high school group's going out for Chinese food. I'll be leaving Monday," he explained to Garth, "but I'll see you in the fall, I hope."

He held up a hand in salute. "Talk to you soon, Kris," he called. As he disappeared down the stairs she was sure his smile seemed strained. But he'd been under a lot of pressure lately. Who wouldn't seem a little strained?

"Nice guy," Garth commented.

"He really is," Kris agreed. "Exactly what he seems."

He pointed to the door. "How about it? I know a place in the Marina where the ice cream's legendary."

Kris' eyes crinkled in a smile. The summer dusk had softened the city's outline, and the breeze blowing off the Bay felt cool on her face.

"It's warm in here!" she exclaimed, cranking open the windows after snapping on the living room lights. "Heat in San Francisco always catches me by surprise. In Willows I expect it, but not in San Francisco." She stuck a finger into the soil of her drooping Boston fern.

Garth called from the kitchen. "I've found the best place in your apartment—in front of the freezer! I'll put the ice cream inside till we're ready for it."

"The bowls are in the cupboard to the right of the sink.

I'm going to take a minute to mist this fern—heat's so hard on it." She sprayed a fine mist over every leaf of the huge fern.

"Garth," she called, "did you have supper? I'll be glad to fix us something more substantial."

She walked into the bright kitchen as he scooped final layers onto two mountains of coconut ice cream. "On second thought," she laughed, "that'll be enough!"

He licked the spoon, looking like a very large little boy. "Coconut ice cream on a summer night. What more could we want?"

Kris opened a drawer. "Spoons, maybe?" Then she pointed to a cupboard. "And would you grab a couple napkins from in there?"

After agreeing it was the best ice cream she'd ever had, Kris looked over at him, her spoon in midair. "Now . . . you had some questions?"

"Okay, I'll get right to it. You know I've been going to the Bible study in radiology?"

"You mentioned that. Still like it?"

"It's outstanding. I've learned a lot—and I had no idea so many University staff were Christians."

"Discovering that someone you've known for a while is a believer is sort of like unwrapping a present, isn't it?"

"That's exactly it." He dug a small road up his mountain of ice cream with the tip of his spoon. "I know I'm growing in my faith, Kris. We're memorizing Scripture, and that's a challenge I like. I'm afraid my question's pretty basic." He hesitated. "That's why I'm asking you—I don't want to reveal my ignorance at the Bible study."

"Okay, Doctor, let's hear it. I promise not to laugh."

"It's that little phrase 'quiet time' I hear so often. 'God showed me this in my quiet time.' 'During my quiet time I felt strongly that—' " He shook his head. "What are they talking about?"

"It does sort of sound like the reading room at the library, doesn't it? Actually, it's just a phrase some Christians use to describe a daily time alone with God. It can be in the morning, evening, whatever."

"Do you have a quiet time?" he asked, scraping his bowl.

"Sure do. Morning works best for me. I get up twenty minutes early to make sure I get it in."

"And what do you do?"

"Well, it's sort of my day's spiritual meal. We eat enough food each day for twenty-four hours, not for a whole week. It's the same spiritually—to keep a healthy relationship with God, we've got to feed on His Word each day."

"I like that," Garth said slowly. "I've been studying the Bible as if there's no tomorrow. So many things have fallen into place for me through what I've learned, but I don't have any system or order about when I study. And I can't always count on getting to church—emergencies aren't scheduled. A planned time with God has a lot of appeal."

"Once it's really a habit, you'll be lost without it."

"So you read for about twenty minutes?"

"No, I only read Scripture for about half that time. The other half I spend in prayer. For my day, for Grandma, my patients, anything on my mind."

Garth's eyes smiled at her, half-teasing. "I'm pretty familiar with the book of Philippians, myself . . . especially that part about anxiety. Remember the sermon the first day I came to church? About worry, and leaving it in God's hands?" He looked across the kitchen. "That day didn't end at all the way I'd hoped, Kris. After you left, I . . . well, let's just say I got acquainted with God's advice about anxiety."

For the second time that evening Kris felt her cheeks flame. The memory of his kiss was still as vivid as though it had happened yesterday.

"It had been a very full day. I think we both were tired," she stammered.

He closed one hand over hers, pushing the dishes away with the other.

"Garth, please. . . ."

"Kris, what is it?" His hazel eyes were serious and he made no effort to remove his hand. "I feel as if you're one of my very best friends. I can talk to you about almost anything. You're an outstanding nurse, and you're great to be with." He leaned closer, frowning. "But at the same time I don't know you at all. You only let me get so near, and then you run. You run away somewhere I can't follow. Why, Kris?"

Panic clutched at her throat and she jerked her hand away. "This is ridiculous," she muttered. "I don't know what you're talking about. Why don't I make us some coffee?"

She walked blindly across the kitchen and yanked open the cupboard where neat rows of ceramic mugs hung from small brass hooks. She stared at them, unseeing. Then she sensed Garth beside her and saw his hand reach over and close the cupboard door.

"Kris." His voice was gentler than she'd ever heard it. "Kris, no. I don't want anything right now, except for us to be honest with each other. This has to be faced. You're afraid of something, afraid to let anyone get too close."

"You'll find out sooner or later I'm not afraid of anything," she shot back, her voice trembling with fear and anger. "Most of all you!"

He ignored her outburst. "Know what I think, Kris? I think you're afraid of your own feelings." Quiet filled the room. "I think you're afraid to love."

"Love?" She laughed, a high-pitched, brittle laugh that sounded strange even to her. "Garth, we're friends, remember? That's what it has to be. Friends."

"That's what you say it has to be. Why only friends, Kris?"

"It's . . . it's just better that way." She swallowed hard, though her mouth felt dry. He mustn't see the hollow place inside her. He mustn't ever know. If she could just stay in control, keep things light, at least then they'd stay friends.

For several minutes he stood quietly beside her. Then he walked back to the table and sat down. When he looked up he was smiling.

"Would you mind sitting down? Please?"

She sat uneasily on the edge of a chair. They'd come to her apartment to answer his questions. How had it turned into this?

"Kris, I've got some people I'd like you to meet. Some people I think you'd enjoy."

Instantly the panic returned. Sybil was the only one of his friends she'd met, but that was enough. She didn't need any more. Grandma was right about not getting too familiar with people . . . people who weren't their kind.

"I don't think so." She shook her head. "It's better if we see each other at work, or church, and let it go at that."

"I'm talking about my parents. I think if you knew them you'd understand. I'd really like you to meet them."

Kris smiled. Now he was being polite, trying to make up for this horrible conversation.

"I'm sure they're wonderful," she answered, feeling her panic ebb like a low tide. "Maybe someday we'll meet." This daydream of his she could handle, because it would never happen.

"They're great. And they'd like you. I'll work on it, Kris." He checked his watch. "Nine-thirty. I'd better get going."

She stood up immediately and led him to the door. "Hope I answered your question, at least a little."

He looked down at her, his eyes gold and chestnut in the lamplight. "You answered one question, but not all of them. Not by a long shot." He smoothed a curl away from her cheek, brushing her skin with his hand. "But friends we are, Miss Carothers . . . friends we are."

She closed the door behind him and stood by the kitchen window, watching the twinkling lights of the quieting city. Over and over the memory of their talk replayed in her mind. Could he possibly be right? Could she be afraid of her feelings? Could she be afraid to love? Of course not. Not the right man. But that man was not Garth Endicott.

12

THE DOORBELL RANG AT FIVE-THIRTY on the dot. Kris buttoned a white culotte skirt around her waist and adjusted her pink knit shirt. After slipping new off-the-rack sunglasses into her purse she locked the door, marveling at what a shower, lemon splash, and a change of clothes could do for someone who had left work only half an hour ago.

She'd been looking forward to this long, relaxing evening with Todd, to deepening their special friendship. He'd come to her mind more and more frequently of late, and she was beginning to view their secure, stable relationship in a new light. No fireworks went off when they were together, but in the long run maybe that was better than rockets and sparklers.

She hurried down the white concrete stairs, welcoming the brush of the late afternoon breeze on her skin. Todd waited for her in a blue-green shirt that turned his eyes to turquoise.

"Hi, Kris. You look wonderful! You did work today, didn't you?"

"I sure did," she laughed. "But thanks for the compliment!"

He turned down the radio of his white Ford Escort and pulled into the heavy Friday afternoon traffic. "Hungry?"

"As usual. The whole week was wild. It really helped to look forward to a lazy evening together."

Todd shifted in his seat. "I'm afraid our evening isn't going to be quite what I'd hoped."

"All the pizza places go out of business?" she joked, enjoying tantalizing glimpses of the sunlit Bay.

"I wish it were that simple. It's all these arrangements for the trip." He negotiated a left turn and headed in the general direction of North Beach. "I'm afraid I have to be back at church for a meeting tonight."

"A meeting on Friday night? What time?"

"Starts at seven-thirty."

"Todd, that's awful," she told him, unable to hide her disappointment. "I was so hoping we'd have some time to talk."

"I don't like it either, but that was honestly the only opening we could find. The kids wanted this last weekend with their parents, and I don't blame them. So tonight was it."

"What's on your agenda?"

"Kind of a wrap-up. We'll be going over everything about the trip. Departure times, plans once we arrive, evangelism strategy, emergency contacts, the works." He slowed the car as they passed crowded sidewalk art galleries, intriguing restaurants of every nationality, and inviting, informal shops. Finally he turned into the parking lot of a one-story redwood building.

"Mama Zia's!" Kris exclaimed, touched by his thoughtfulness. "I haven't been here for ages—since you brought me right after I arrived in San Francisco. Remember?"

"I sure do. You were green as grass to the city, and I wasn't much better. Thought you might enjoy it, even though we don't have the time I'd hoped for."

"Well, we'll make the most of what we do have. I've never forgotten their pizza." She hoped she sounded pleased. Even at this hour she felt his tension, certain that he was watching the time.

He was always in a hurry and they never had time to talk any more. Did he know about this meeting all along? Was that why he suggested coming at five-thirty, to keep their date short?

They found a corner table covered with a red and white checkered tablecloth, and for a while Kris forgot her nagging questions. They split a bread stick from a napkin-lined basket and studied the menu together.

"Well, what'll it be?" Todd smiled at her. "Two salads and a medium pizza with everything, especially pineapple? I think that's what we had before."

Kris folded up the menu. "Sounds great. And a diet Coke." She turned her head, listening. "The music in here's beautiful—I'd forgotten."

Todd gave their order to a young man whose ponytail hung below his shoulder blades, then turned his attention to the restaurant's background music. "I think that's Puccini."

"Puccini? I didn't know you knew anything about opera, or even liked it."

"These days I don't have any time for it, but I've always enjoyed it. Puccini wrote some of the most exquisite operatic music in the world. How about you? Do you like opera?"

"Well, to be honest, I've never paid any attention to it. But if this music's any example, maybe I'd enjoy it." Uneasy, she sipped her Coke.

Garth and his family went to the opera regularly. But Dad and Grandma never had money, let alone interest, for such things. Kris had always dismissed opera and the theater as amusements of the wealthy. But maybe . . .

"Excuse me. Who had Roquefort?" asked the waiter.

"Roquefort here, house dressing there," Todd answered. The waiter set down the salads and left.

"This looks great," Todd said. "Why don't we thank God for it?" He reached across the table for her hand, and they bowed their heads. "Thanks, Father. You're so good. Bless our conversation. Help us to love You more, for Jesus' sake."

Kris snapped another bread stick in half. "Getting excited about leaving? Only three more days." She looked up, eager to leave opera behind.

"I am, and so are the kids. It'll give all of us a real opportunity for shoe-leather Christianity. There's quite a difference between a plush office in the States and what we'll find in Zimbabwe. We'll have a chance to put our faith into action."

"When do you come back?"

"The third week in August. The kids need time to sort of decompress and get ready for school."

"That's two months, Todd." Kris stared at him, coming to grips with how long he'd be away. How different everything would be without him.

"I know. But it'll go by fast. You'll see."

The waiter reappeared with a bubbling pizza covered with creamy cheese, broiled to a golden brown. Tantalizing bits of pepperoni, mushrooms, salami, pineapple, and green peppers peeked shyly from their blanket of mozzarella. Todd fought his way into the thick first slice, swirling escaping tendrils of cheese away from the pan.

Kris watched, only half aware of what he was doing. "Do you know where you'll be staying? I want to write you."

He handed her a small plate holding two slices of pizza. "Kris, I've prayed and I've thought about that so much." He spoke slowly, as though choosing each word with great care. "There's nothing I'd like more than to hear from you." He looked away, molding a paper napkin into a compressed cube. "But I . . . I'm going to ask you not to write."

Chapter Twelve

"Not write? Why?" Her stomach felt exactly the way it had back in high school, on the day they posted the names of the new cheerleaders.

Suzie Calloway . . . Jeri Finch. . . . Her eyes skated up and down the paper, searching for her name, but it was nowhere on the list. She went directly to the cheerleader advisor, positive she'd done her routines well.

It wasn't her ability, Miss Perkins reassured her. She had lots of that. But there was the mandatory cheerleading camp, winter and spring uniforms to buy, and all the other expenses. They were aware, Miss Perkins said kindly, that such things might put a strain on Kris's family. The judges felt it would be kinder to end it now.

She didn't argue, ashamed that even the teachers knew how poor the Carothers family was. So every Friday afternoon she pretended to be swamped with chemistry experiments. But from the shelter of the lab's half-drawn curtains she watched the bus drive away, loaded with uniformed players and giggling cheerleaders.

Now once again something she longed for was speeding away, leaving her powerless to stop it.

"Kris, I know what I'm saying seems unfair," Todd was saying. "But I think we need to put our relationship on hold for a while. We need to give ourselves time to discover God's will for each of us . . . and for our friendship." He squeezed a napkin wad with nervous fingers as he talked.

"Todd!" Kris laughed impatiently, fighting a surge of anger. "This doesn't make sense! Less than two months ago you told me—"

"I know . . . but a lot's changed since then."

"Like what?" She pushed away her cold pizza, interested only in unraveling the snarled strands of their relationship.

"Kris, I'm changing. So are you. It's true that God gave us a beautiful friendship. We've enriched each other, and it's helped us grow. But isn't it possible that God gave us each other for a certain time in our lives? And that our friendship wasn't necessarily meant to evolve into anything deeper?" He looked down at his hands.

Todd had always been someone she could count on, no matter what. He was like family. They were from the same kind of people, they liked the same kinds of things. But tonight he was saying something new. Not only was he leaving, but . . .

Hurt, confused, and suddenly frightened, Kris looked over at him. "Todd . . . are you saying good-bye?"

He grabbed her hand. "Of course not, Kris! What was it C.S. Lewis said? 'Christians never say good-bye!' I'm just saying we need to give each other some time and space." He released her hand. "We each need to see what God has for us, and not rush ahead of Him." He slid another piece of pizza onto her plate.

"I agree with that part. It's just . . . this is such a shock."

When he looked up there was a flicker of pain in Todd's clear blue eyes. "I don't want to say any more right now. But as I've prayed and thought about it, Kris, I'm convinced we need time apart."

"Is that why you're going to Zimbabwe?"

He smiled. "No. God's calling me there—that's one thing I'm sure of. But I believe He provided it now partly because of what I've been telling you. We'll never know what we feel if one of us doesn't leave for a while, Kris."

"Then I won't hear from you till the end of summer?"

He looked directly at her. "That's right. I know I've hurt you, and I feel terrible about that. But I believe it's best this way."

She looked at her half-eaten dinner. "I'm trying to understand. . . ."

"Trust me. A lot's going on in your life, and in mine. God may show us we have a future together. And He may show us our friendship will remain just that. But Kris, you know how much you mean to me, how hard this is." He looked away.

She'd always respected him, and as she listened to him that respect deepened. She could learn to love him, no question about it. But was that God's best for them? Hard as it was to admit, deep inside she knew Todd was right. Their friendship had grown over the years they'd known each other, but during the past few months it seemed to stand still. Something held her back, something she couldn't define.

Maybe Garth was right after all. Maybe she really was afraid to get close to people. Without looking she sensed Todd checking his watch, and reeled in her racing thoughts.

"Kris, I'm sorry. It's seven-fifteen. I'm afraid we need to get going."

She slipped her purse over her shoulder and tried to smile. "It was a delicious dinner. Guess I wasn't as hungry as I thought."

"I didn't help much."

They drove to her apartment in preoccupied silence. Kris watched the deepening twilight blanket the city, and thought about home. There, instead of the traffic's constant roar, she'd hear the pulsing rhythm of giant irrigation pumps watering the vast fields. It all seemed so far away, like another world.

"What are you thinking about?"

"Oh, home, and Grandma. Nothing deep."

"Are you unhappy here?"

"Not really, I guess. I don't know. I love Willows so much, and the life I had there. Everything was so simple. But sometimes I wish I could have grown up differently. Maybe traveled. Experienced more."

"Like opera?"

She was suddenly on guard. "That's an odd remark."

"Just wondering." He pulled up to the curb outside her apartment, shut off the motor, and looked straight at her. "Kris, trust God's leading. Don't fight Him. He doesn't make mistakes, you know."

She felt like a little girl being scolded. "Of course I know." But as he circled the car to her door, she wondered what he meant. What a strange evening it had turned out to be.

"Wish you could come in," she said wistfully as they walked to her apartment door. "But I guess you need to hurry."

"I really do." He waited as she searched for her key, his sandy hair tinged with red by the apartment's outside light.

She knew things would never be the same between them. "If you change your mind about writing—"

"Let's keep it the way it is, Kris. It's better left in God's hands." He gave her a quick smile and disappeared down the stairs.

Kris waited in the doorway until the sound of his car faded away. Then she locked the door and leaned against it, overwhelmed by a pervasive sadness. Becoming Todd's wife would be so easy . . . so familiar. But everything he'd said made sense.

What's wrong with me, Lord? she whispered. *Why is it all so complicated? Where do I belong? Who am I, Lord?*

The phone rang and Kris felt her way through the dark apartment to the kitchen. She hesitated before picking it up, remembering the frightening phone game a few weeks ago and wondering if she should answer.

"Hello?"

"Hi, honey. Been tryin' to get ahold of you for a couple of hours!"

"Grandma! Oh, I'm so happy you called!" Kris flipped on the light and sat down, relieved at the sound of the dear, familiar voice. "Grandma, is everything all right?"

"Of course, child. That big rent check you sent me came. Makes me feel bad, takin' your money every month. And you've been on my mind. How're things goin', dear?"

"Oh, work is fine. We're slowly getting the kinks out of life in the new Pavilion."

"How 'bout when you're not workin'?"

"Oh. . . . Well, I guess I wrote you about Mandie and Hank. They're getting more and more excited about trying to adopt a baby. Keep praying for them, won't you?"

"Every day, and that's a promise. How's that young man you think so much of . . . Todd?" Grandma had made no secret of the fact she thought a minister would make an ideal husband.

"Oh, he's fine, Grandma." Kris tried to keep her tone casual. "In fact, we had dinner together tonight."

"And you're home already?"

Exactly how I feel, Kris thought. "Well, he had a meeting. In two days he's leaving for a mission project in Zimbabwe, South Africa."

"I knew by your voice somethin' was wrong, honey. Now, I don't want to meddle, but if it'd help to talk. . . ."

Just listening to her grandmother's depth of concern made her feel better. "Oh, I'll be all right, Grandma. Tonight was sort of hard, and . . . I don't know. Guess I've been a little homesick, to tell the truth."

"Oh, honey. You comin' home?" Excitement twinkled in every word.

Kris laughed. "No . . . not yet. We're so busy at work, I couldn't leave if I wanted to. And I need to kind of sift things out. I love San Francisco, but it's so different from Willows. Sometimes I feel like someone from another planet in this city. Does that make any sense, Grandma?"

"Honey, it makes lots of sense. And it starts me to thinkin' about a quilt I'm workin' on for the fall bazaar. Wedding Ring. Remember it?"

"Oh, yes! With all the little pieces? It's so beautiful."

"That's the one. And it's beautiful, all right, but it don't get that way overnight. Not on your life. I'm buildin' it piece by piece, block by block. It'll take months just to put together, and then there's still all the quiltin' . . . stitch by stitch.

"And honey, life's like that. Our heavenly Father's quiltin' on our lives, one stitch at a time. Sometimes we feel pulled up tighter'n a bastin' thread, but He knows what He's doin'. I think maybe He's got you on a tight thread right now, Krissy. But you keep your hand tight in His. Keep on trustin' Him. He knows what He's doin', honey."

Kris's eyes misted with tears. Grandma's way of looking at the world could always make things right again . . . because Grandma saw everything in life through the eyes of faith.

"Oh, Grandma. I feel better already! I think maybe I just needed a good dose of you!"

"I'm glad, dear. Now tell me, are you seein' anyone besides this Todd? What about that doctor fella you wrote about . . . the one who runs that Pavilion of yours?"

"Well, he doesn't quite run it," she laughed, surprised Grandma would be interested in anyone but Todd. "But he is the medical director there, and one of the best pediatricians I've ever worked with. We're good friends, that's all."

"You ever step out with him?"

"Well . . . he's shown me some of the city. But it's nothing special. He loves to show off San Francisco. He was born in this city."

"Must know it pretty good, then."

Kris thought of Sakamoto's Sushi restaurant, and Coit Tower, and Golden Gate Park. "He does, Grandma. He knows places I never dreamed existed."

Grandma didn't answer right away, and Kris could almost hear her thinking.

"Well, honey, you keep rememberin' that quilt. It takes a long time to get all those pieces fit together just so. I'll keep prayin' and you keep trustin'. Now I gotta go. Call you when some news happens."

"Grandma, thanks for calling! I love you."

As always, Grandma hung up the moment she decided the conversation was over. But even then Kris knew her life and feelings were being lifted before the Lord, because Grandma talked almost nonstop to God in prayer.

She took a long, relaxing breath, then walked to the bay window and looked out at the bustling city. The evening had turned out pretty well after all.

13

ANY WORD FROM SURGERY?"

For a moment Kris forgot the computer's supply order file. "Nothing yet . . . but Kyung's only been up there an hour and a half. It'll be two, probably three hours before we know much." Mandie knew all that as well as anyone, but for some reason today she seemed to need to hear it from someone else. "How're things down at your end?"

"Fine. Two of 'em are asleep, but little Pete's pretty unhappy. He's the one with the fracture reduction, and does he hate that cast! Fifteen months old, nobody will let him walk, and he's mad at the world!"

Mandie's brown eyes crinkled in a brief smile that soon faded. "I hope Kyung Lee can take this operation, Kris. It takes all the energy she has just to drink milk from a bottle."

"How did she seem this morning, before her preop meds?"

"Listless, as always. She didn't even cry when the ICU nurses hooked up her lines. Just watched with those big black eyes. Of course, it's the atrial-septal defect. Her blood's so oxygen hungry she doesn't have strength for anything except basic survival."

Kris pulled Kyung's chart from the rack and flipped to the diagnostic reports. "She's got a classic atrial-septal defect, and that ASD is large." She accentuated the last word, reviewing the baby's test results. "Cardiac catheterization, echocardiogram, electrocardiogram, blood work-up, presenting symptoms. Everything confirms the diagnosis."

"I know," Mandie sighed. "She can't live without this surgery. But I pray she won't have to be on the heart-lung machine long. Let me know the minute you hear something?"

"I promise."

"I've never seen her so worked up about a patient, Kris," Carmen said as soon as Mandie moved beyond earshot.

"She's really worried. There's something about that baby." Kris checked her watch. "I'd better take my break while I can—I'll be in the lounge."

"I'll call if anything comes up. Now get going before something does!"

Kris laughed. Without Carmen's good-natured prodding she'd never get a break.

The smell of fresh-brewed coffee welcomed her into the lounge. She filled her blue mug and sat down, stretching her legs across the vinyl couch. As usual the late coffee break was a mixed blessing—no one to talk to, but a wonderfully restful silence.

She leaned back and reviewed the events of the weekend. It was surprising how relaxed she felt, given the disastrous dinner with Todd Friday night. By now he was probably on his way. How strange it would be not to talk to him, not to see him at church, not even to write. But Grandma's call had been just what she'd needed, and the rest of the weekend had turned out all right.

It had been good to attend the play therapy seminar on Saturday and learn how children of all ages could be encouraged to act out their hidden feelings through puppets, drawings, stories, and songs. And it was helpful to share problems and ideas with other pediatric nurses from the city's hospitals. She made a mental note to discuss with Mr. Talbot the possibility of hiring a third play therapist.

Sunday had been foggy, a perfect day for an after-church minestrone soup and French bread lunch at Mandie and Hank's. Thinking about it now made her hungry.

The phone in the lounge rang and Kris grabbed it. Nobody would interrupt a nurse's break except for an emergency.

"This is Miss Carothers."

"Hi, Kris—Carmen. Sorry to bother you, but I think we've got a problem."

"Be right there." In less than a minute she had joined Carmen at the nurses' station entrance.

"What's up? Did surgery call?"

"No word from surgery, but this does concern Kyung. You know Lily Castillo, who was going to do Kyung's foster care?"

"Was going to?"

"Her husband phoned while you were gone. She's just learned she has mononucleosis. There's no way Kyung can stay there."

"Poor Lily," Kris answered. "She does a lot of foster care."

"Well, for a while they'll be stopping all of it. Doctor's orders. So what do we do about Kyung?"

"If everything goes the way it should, she'll be discharged in five to seven days. You'd better get in touch with Mr. Talbot right away. Maybe he can contact Operation Search about alternate care."

Mandie reappeared in time to catch the last few words. "What's up? Kyung's all right, isn't she?"

"She's fine," Kris assured her. "At least we haven't heard

otherwise. The problem is her foster care. The woman scheduled to take care of her has mono."

"Could Hank and I take her?"

Kris stared at her friend, wondering if she'd heard right. "You and Hank? Your vacation starts next week, Mandie. You're going backpacking in the Sierras, remember?"

"We can do that another time. Hank's home right now—do you mind if I ask him?" Mandie's eyes were black with intensity.

"You nut. Of course not!" Kris laughed. "I'm just in shock, that's all. I can't imagine anything better for Kyung, but I hate to see you and Hank give up your plans. Still . . . "

Kris realized they were both playing games. For Hank and Mandie, no vacation in the world could compare with the joy of having a baby in the house, even it were only for a few weeks. And Kris knew better than anyone the kind of love and attention they could give—she'd been the recipient of that love more times than she could count.

"Good. I'll call from the pay phone—it's more private." Mandie almost ran down the hall.

Carmen whistled a soft, joyful note. "Dear Lord, touch that man's heart!" Carmen prayed. "Shall I hold off calling Mr. Talbot?"

"Yes. And keep praying!"

A few minutes later Mandie reappeared at the nursing station, her eyes sparkling. "He's all for it. What's it take to get licensed for foster care?"

"He didn't mind giving up the vacation?"

"Says he'd rather clean a baby than a fish any day," Mandie laughed. "We can always go camping," she added, suddenly serious. "But babies like Kyung only come around once in a lifetime. If we can help get her off to a good start, well. . . ."

Gently Kris touched her friend's arm. "Mandie, she has to go back to Korea when she's well. That'll be difficult.

Are you sure you want to do this?"

"I know. We realize she'll have to leave. And it helps knowing how definite that is. We'll give her the best start possible, and keep reminding ourselves she's only visiting." She took a deep breath. "And this will help get us ready for the real thing."

"That's all I wanted to hear. Carmen, get Mr. Talbot on the phone, would you? I want to talk to him before he goes to lunch. Speaking of lunch, what about yours, Mandie?"

"My appetite's gone! Hank's calling his sister right now. Their third is two years old, so maybe we can use some of their baby stuff."

"Kris?" Carmen broke in. "Mr. Talbot, line three."

Kris took the phone. "Hi, Mr. Talbot. Yes, that's right, mononucleosis. We were ready to call you when Mandie Dixon and her husband, Hank, offered to take the baby." She smiled. "I agree. The finest!" She listened for several more moments. "I'll tell her. She'll be here all afternoon if you need her for anything. Thanks, Mr. Talbot." Kris hung up and turned to Mandie.

"Your offer is the best possible thing we could give Kyung. He's very grateful, Mandie. He's calling the social service worker now. Wants to see how fast they can license you and Hank."

"D'you think there'll be any problem?"

Kris laughed. "None. They'll probably make you sign a paper promising not to change your mind! Mr. Talbot said he'll call back this afternoon."

"All right. I'm going upstairs for a cup of tea. I need to collect my thoughts. Any chance you could get away?"

Kris checked her watch. "I just had a late break—still need to finish ordering supplies. And I've been trying to vary the time I go up. Less chance of running into Dr. Burack. You go ahead. I'll call if we get any news."

Looking slightly dazed, Mandie hurried to the elevator.

*C*HAPTER *T*HIRTEEN

As Kris returned to the computer's order form, the lilting words of a praise song filled her heart to overflowing. "Praise You, Father . . . Bless You, Jesus . . . Thank You, Holy Spirit, for being here, being here. . . ."

WHILE GARTH, MANDIE, AND Kyung Lee's social worker discussed details of her outpatient care, Kris looked appreciatively around the parents' waiting area where they had all met. The quiet cheerfulness struck her every time she came in. The soothing blues and yellows contrasted with the panorama of the city, framed by enormous picture windows.

Across from Kris sat Connie O'Malley, for years a University Hospital social worker. She patiently answered Mandie's many questions, her short gray hair framing a face always on the verge of a smile.

"I'm so glad you could come on such short notice, Connie," Kris said, moving to the edge of the comfortable blue sofa. "We only heard about Lily's illness a few hours before Kyung came back from surgery."

"I'd planned to be in my office all day anyhow. Right now every foster family we have is at load limit. So when Mr. Talbot called with this news, I wanted to talk to Amanda and Dr. Endicott right away."

"Connie doesn't think we'll have any problem getting a temporary license, Kris," Mandie added, studying a pocket calendar. "We've set up an appointment for her to come out to the house."

Connie flipped through the stack of papers on her lap. "We'll make that a top priority. All we need is a partial home study, and I certainly don't anticipate any problems with that." She turned to Garth. "If the recovery goes smoothly, Dr. Endicott, how soon could the baby be discharged?"

Garth pulled a small bulging notebook from his plaid

shirt pocket. "Probably about a week from today. Surgery went well. The cardiologist and the cardiac surgeon both agree that, barring complications, she should be well before we know it."

"Then I'd better get back to my office and start the ball rolling!" Connie hoisted a tailored navy blue carrying case over one shoulder. "Mandie, I'm so glad this has worked out. I'll look forward to seeing you and Hank on Wednesday. Kris, thanks. I'll be in touch in a day or two."

The moment Connie left the room, Mandie faced Kris and Garth, her dark brown eyes filled with wonder. "I can't believe it! All this came up less than three hours ago, and there hasn't been one problem so far." Her face crinkled in a smile. "Speaking of problems, I wonder how Hank's doing moving baby furniture!"

"If I know Hank, it's all under control," Kris replied. "Garth, I checked on Kyung after she got back to ICU. How do you feel she's doing?"

"Surgery took about five hours," he replied. "She's still pretty groggy. She'll stay on the respirator for a few days, of course, to ease the demand on her heart. But things went very smoothly."

"Was she on the heart-lung machine long?" Mandie asked.

"About an hour and a half," Garth replied. "That's pretty good, considering the size of her septal defect. That pediatric heart surgery staff is incredible," he said slowly. "I never get used to their skill with those little patients."

"Garth, I've been looking everywhere for you! Don't tell me you forgot our little meeting?"

As one, three heads turned to the entry of the parents' waiting area. Nobody talked that way except Sybil.

She had swept her auburn hair away from her face, making her look at once childlike and sophisticated. A low-cut, turquoise silk blouse under a two-piece ecru suit emphasized her emerald eyes. Her long legs shimmered in light silk hose and fragile, bone-colored sandals.

Stunning, Kris thought grudgingly. *She looks absolutely stunning.*

Sybil remained poised in the doorway, ignoring everyone but Garth, obviously relishing their stares. "I hope I'm not interrupting anything important," she murmured in a honeyed voice.

"It's all right. We were about finished," Garth muttered. "Uh . . . what meeting . . . ?"

"Dr. Garth Endicott!" Sybil was visibly exasperated. "It's for the fall fund-raiser, remember? That nice little man from the Mark Hopkins Hotel is here to go over details. The woman from I. Magnin's came, too. They're all downstairs, waiting for us."

"I'll be there right away. Where is it?"

Her eyes grew even larger. "You did you say we could use the conference room, didn't you?"

"I don't remember anything about—Okay." He scratched the back of his neck. "Call me if anything comes up, Kris. Conference room." He looked sheepish and seemed to take more time than necessary to put away his notebook. "Be back tonight, after dinner."

In three long steps he reached the door and disappeared with Sybil. The staccato click of her high heels faded, blending with the afternoon sounds of the Pavilion.

As she left the parents' waiting room, Kris thought of Garth's face as he'd pushed his notebook back into his pocket. How could he let her make such a fool of him? What could a man like Garth Endicott possibly see in a woman like Sybil Trefts?

As they neared the nurses' station, Mandie broke the thoughtful silence.

"Wonder if Sybil ever thought of buying a sterling silver leash for him—one that folds up into a handy purse size?"

Their laughter relieved the tension, but Kris was preoccupied all afternoon. Women were nothing new to Garth, that was for sure. And it was definitely none of her concern. But why did he allow Sybil to lead him around like a pedigreed puppy? Could that possibly be Garth Endicott's idea of love?

14

HOW'S EVERYTHING COMING on this special day?" Kris stood in the doorway to LeRoy Jones's room, her lemon yellow uniform reflecting her joy. Today LeRoy was finally going home.

"Good morning, Miss Carothers!" His mother lowered a stack of puzzles and books onto the window seat. "I wonder if you'd happen to have any extra sacks around? This boy's got so many toys it'll take a moving truck to get him out of here!" The soaring happiness in her voice filled every corner of the room.

"Dozens. I'll send some down right away." Kris walked to LeRoy's bedside, circling the rocking chair and a box bulging with stuffed animals. "How're you doing, champ? All ready for the big event?"

LeRoy sat cross-legged in the middle of the bed wearing a white football jersey, blue jeans, and brand new Reebok pumps. An orange and black Giants baseball cap hid his total hair loss. Though still pale and seven pounds thinner than when he arrived, lately everything LeRoy did reflected unmistakable signs of increasing strength. Two weeks ago he would have chosen to lie down, not sit. His eyes would have looked dull and clouded with fatigue, not shining.

"Hey, Miss Carothers," he said, giving her a high-five. "Guess where we're going when I get out of here?" His voice cracked with excitement.

"Tell me." Kris's eyes were riveted to LeRoy's.

"The pound!"

"The what?"

"The pound. I'm getting a puppy! Any kind I want in the whole place!"

"Oh, LeRoy, that's wonderful!" Kris fought back tears, awed by his pure delight. "What kind do you want?"

"One that's warm and wiggles and licks my face!"

Kris glanced at his mother. "I don't imagine that'll be too hard to find, do you, Mrs. Jones?"

Their eyes met in silent understanding. "Not hard at all. There's a puppy out there just waiting to come live with LeRoy! His Dad's going with us . . . using his lunch break to help his boy pick out that dog."

"Are we almost ready, Mom?"

"Almost ready, son. I need to fold up your robe."

"Has Dr. Endicott stopped by yet, Mrs. Jones?"

"He was here around eight. Said someone would be back in a little while to explain about the outpatient clinic."

"I'll go find him. And I'll bring those sacks back myself, so you can get out of here. Mustn't keep that puppy waiting!"

Kris's heart sang she walked down the corridor. LeRoy's body had given a textbook response to University Hospital's aggressive treatment for Hodgkin's disease. All the staff were optimistic about his complete recovery.

A light was on in Garth's office and Kris knocked on the open door.

"I don't know what's giving off more sunshine," Garth

said, looking up from a stack of charts, "your yellow uniform or that smile of yours." He tossed his pen onto the pile of papers and leaned back. "What's made you so happy?"

"LeRoy Jones is ready to go home, and he's about to pop from the excitement. Guess where his mom's taking him after they leave here?"

"McDonald's?"

"No!" Kris laughed. "They're going straight to the pound to pick out a puppy."

"That's beautiful. A new start for a puppy, and a new start for LeRoy."

But Kris had the distinct impression his thoughts were way ahead of the conversation.

"They're about ready to go," she continued. "Mrs. Jones is just waiting for instructions on outpatient care."

"I'd like him seen in the Hematology/Oncology Clinic a week from today. Soon as that's set up he can walk out the door."

"We'll take care of it. Now to get some sacks for his toys."

"Kris, wait a second. Are you by any chance free this afternoon?"

"I think so. Why?"

"I'd like to take you somewhere." Something in his voice reminded Kris of LeRoy talking about his puppy.

"What time?"

"Right after work. Can you make it?"

"Of course. Where should I meet you?"

"In the lobby, near the door. Around four?"

"I'll be there." She hurried back to LeRoy's room, stopping by the utility room to pick up the sacks. Whatever Garth wanted, she had a feeling, was important. And it probably wouldn't take long. Then she remembered that he always met Sybil at four o'clock. Maybe Sybil was going to drag them around on a tour of hotel dining rooms for her fund-raiser.

GARTH WAS WAITING WHEN she stepped into the hospital lobby at ten after four. As soon as she saw him she wished she'd taken time to at least put on some lipstick.

"Sorry I'm late."

"No problem. Car's around to the side."

Kris shivered and pulled her sweater around her as they started up the sidewalk. During the day a damp summer fog had settled over the city, eclipsing the sun. It was a relief to get into the warm car.

The more she'd thought about it during the afternoon, the more convinced Kris had become that they were off to a meeting with Sybil Trefts. As Garth backed out of the doctors' parking area, Kris tried to discover more about their destination.

"Is the meeting far from here?"

"Meeting?"

"Aren't we meeting with Sybil about the fund-raiser?"

He turned left from the parking lot and worked his way into the right-hand lane. "Sorry. No meeting." Garth laughed as he maneuvered through the heavy afternoon traffic. "You look so worried, Kris. Just trust me for a few minutes. We're almost there."

"I'll try." Nothing about the area they were driving through looked familiar. Almost all the buildings were old, many in need of repair. Children played everywhere. Adolescents lounged against street lights, younger ones played hopscotch on cracked sidewalks, others sat alone or in small groups on steep, half-painted apartment steps.

Soon they turned into a parking lot and stopped in front of an old two-story brick building. "YMCA" read the faded blue letters painted on a small white sign hanging over the entrance.

"We're going to the Y?"

"This is it. Coming with me?"

Kris's eyes questioned him as she smoothed a stray curl rejuvenated by the damp fog. They walked up the worn cement steps through the gold-lettered doors of the ancient building.

"Hi, Doc!"

Before the heavy doors closed behind them, Garth was surrounded by a dozen boys of every size, shape, and color. One, over six feet tall and flagpole thin, dribbled a basketball in steady rhythm as he danced from one foot to the other. Kris felt all of them studying her with open curiosity.

"Hi, Spider," Garth said to the tallest boy. "Like you to meet a good friend. Guys, this is Kris Carothers." As he talked, he handed his sport coat to another boy as short as the first was tall. "Thanks, Razor. You guys ready to play?"

For the first time Kris noticed that Garth had on running shoes, baggy slacks, and a faded striped T-shirt.

"Kris, meet the Tigers. They're something else!" He walked into the group of boys, their numbers increased by the arrival of a lanky black and a muscular Oriental. "You guys start warming up. We'll be right in."

The shouting group raced through another set of doors, and Kris caught a glimpse of a huge basketball court. Its polished wooden floor gleamed under bright overhead lights. As the doors closed, a trim, gray-haired woman with a large whistle around her neck walked toward them.

"Hi, Dr. Endicott. As usual, your fan club is waiting."

"Hi, Midge. The boys are getting started now. I'd like you to meet Kris Carothers. Kris, Midge Peterson. She pretty much holds this place together!"

Kris spoke for the first time since leaving the car. "I'm so glad to meet you, Midge. This is quite a place."

"It wouldn't be the same without Dr. Endicott. He's done so much with these boys since he started working with them. He hardly misses a day."

Garth looked uncomfortable. "Come on, Midge."

"Well, it's true. Don't let him tell you anything different, Kris. Good to meet you. Come on down afterwards," she called. "I'm at the end of the hall."

"Garth Endicott," Kris scolded, facing him.

He grinned. "I sort of lied when I said there wasn't a meeting . . . but it wasn't the kind you were thinking of."

She laughed, trying to sort out her thoughts. "Garth, what a great thing to do."

He shrugged. "Almost everything these kids do after school adds up to trouble. Basketball bleeds off that energy, teaches them coordination, how to be part of a team, self-confidence."

The steady pattern of the basketball next door grew louder, and he glanced toward the closed gym doors. "I need to work with these guys for an hour or so," he said. "Do you mind watching us practice? It would mean a lot to the guys. Then I'll shower and we'll go down the street for a snack." Garth stood in front of her, waiting for her answer.

His old shirt and baggy pants reminded her of her father after he'd driven the school bus and worked the farm for fifteen hours. He'd wash up, find Kris, and they'd sit on the front porch until Grandma called them for supper. But they never talked. He was always too tired for that.

She nodded her agreement to Garth, not trusting herself to speak.

"Great! You can wait with Midge when we're through practicing."

The next hour sped by like a recorder on fast-forward. She sat on a narrow wooden bench against a brick wall, a stack of tumbling mats on her right and a giant scoreboard on her left. Fascinated, she watched Garth lead the noisy team through one play after another. Occasionally he called them into a circle to diagram a routine on a green chalkboard at the edge of the court. Three times he stopped a play to work one-on-one with an overweight white boy who gasped for breath as he struggled to run.

She couldn't help thinking back to Friday nights in Willows.

To earn extra money, her father drove a school bus full of high school students to and from each week's game. The smell of ropes, canvas, leather, and sweat hadn't changed. But back then she'd been the bus driver's daughter, secretly wishing his English were better, his nails cleaner.

And she wished that once, just once, she could have worn clothes bought in a store instead of homemade by Grandma. She'd never lacked for things to wear, but Grandma dismissed fashion as worldly. Once she bought yards of brown floral fabric at a third of the original cost, then stayed up half the night sewing Kris a new dress. The next day Lucy Fielding giggled, covered her mouth, and asked Kris if the dress was made out of their old drapes.

She winced, feeling her anguish as though it were yesterday.

"Watch it, Kris!"

She ducked just in time to avoid a ball aimed for her face. Garth ran toward her.

"You all right?" His eyes were bright with concern, his face streaked with sweat.

"I'm fine," she laughed, tossing the ball back onto the court.

"Good. Another few minutes and we'll call it quits."

Garth led the team through warm-down exercises and slow stretches. His words were encouraging and few, the special language men reserve for men.

"Give me five more minutes, Kris. Then we'll go," Garth

called, disappearing with the team through a side door. She walked slowly through the quiet gym and into the hall.

"Kris? Come on down." Midge Peterson waved at Kris from her office doorway.

"Thanks. That was quite an experience!"

"Isn't he something? He's worked with those boys 'til they're one of the best teams in the city. They come out of the woodwork to be coached by Doc Endicott. How about something to drink? Coffee? Or we have a soft drink machine."

"Oh, no, thanks. Garth said something about going down the street afterwards."

Midge laughed. "Oh, yes. Ferguson's Grill. He loves that place. The food there is one of the city's best kept secrets."

"Looks like you're being well taken care of." Garth stood in the doorway, his brown hair still wet from the shower. He had changed into a white knit shirt and blue windbreaker, the sleeves rolled to midforearm. Kris wished she were wearing anything but a uniform.

"Have time to visit Ferguson's?" he asked. "You'd enjoy it."

"So Midge says. I'd like to see it."

They walked the half block to Ferguson's Grill. As Garth turned the wooden screen door's old handle, Kris was sure she wouldn't have found this place on her own in a hundred years. Patterned, Formica-topped tables with upholstered red vinyl seats surrounded the huge grill. They sat down near a window where they could watch the street lights glowing dimly through the pearl-gray fog.

"Hi, Doc. What'll it be?" called a heavyset man in a wrinkled denim apron from his post behind the grill.

Garth looked at Kris. "Hamburger, fries, and salad? Elmer's hamburgers are the best around."

"I only came for coffee, but that sounds delicious!"

"Coming up! Two hamburgers and fries and two dinner salads, Elmer. One tea, one coffee."

"You got it, Doc." Five seconds later they heard hamburgers sizzling on the grill.

Kris leaned forward. "Why haven't you ever mentioned your basketball team? I never dreamed you were doing something like this." She struggled against a strange wave of emotion.

"They're a great bunch of guys. I enjoy every minute of it. Even more since I learned how much God loves those kids, too." He waited while Elmer set two heavy mugs in the middle of the table.

Kris took a sip of her coffee. Maybe she'd misjudged Garth. Some of those afternoon departures could have been for the YMCA . . . but what about all the times she'd seen him leave with Sybil? He couldn't possibly be bringing her to the Y to watch him scrimmage with the team. The image of Sybil in her high heels and crepe de chine dresses sitting on a wooden bench in that smelly gym made her smile.

"Penny for your thoughts, Nurse."

Kris laughed and shook her head. "They'll cost you more than that."

They stopped talking as Elmer set two steaming platters of hamburgers and fries on the table, followed by two wooden bowls of salad.

"Wait till you taste that," Garth said.

Somehow she managed to bite into the two-inch-thick creation and for a while could only nod at Garth. "It's wonderful," she finally managed. "How did you discover this place?"

"San Francisco's full of surprises. You just need the right contacts." His eyes held hers. "Kris, remember I said I wanted you to meet my family?"

Of course she remembered—that night in her kitchen, the night he'd told her she was afraid of her feelings. She looked away, uneasy.

"Well, we're getting together this Saturday at my parents' home. My brothers will be there. Kris, I'd like you to come with me."

A sudden knot of fear took her breath away, like going up in an elevator that stopped too fast. She'd thought Garth was only being polite when he'd mentioned meeting his parents.

The mere thought of meeting them and Garth's brothers was almost more than she could bear. She'd never get through an evening with them. She'd do everything wrong. Use the wrong fork and wrong spoon or say something stupid. They'd see right through her. Grandma always said you couldn't make a silk purse out of a sow's ear.

She looked across the table at Garth. Why did he bother with her? Here she was, wearing a uniform he'd seen dozens of times, her hair wild from the fog, no makeup except ketchup and mustard. Why? He was watching her, his lips curved in a slight smile. What a beautiful mouth he had. She looked down at her dinner, then pushed her plate away. She felt his hand close over hers, his touch warm, filled with that indefinable energy.

"Kris, please come."

She looked up, helpless, her mind numbed by a nameless fear.

"All right. I'll come, but I hope. . . ."

He squeezed her hand. "I'll be there the whole time."

She took a slow, deep breath, and for one brief moment believed she could actually do it.

15

WHERE'LL YOU BE, just in case?" Carmen's words brought Kris up short.

"Carmen, I'm sorry. I'm not thinking. Connie O'Malley needs to talk to Hank and Mandie this morning, and she wants me there. We'll be in the mini-conference room. Shouldn't be long."

Kris hurried to the meeting, exasperated with herself. Today it was impossible to concentrate. Every time she remembered her promise to meet Garth's family she felt cornered. Why had she ever said yes?

Waves of fear drifted in and out of her mind, immobilizing her with dread. Well, tomorrow Garth would see firsthand what she really was. So why was she so upset? Why did she even care what his family thought of her?

Yet she couldn't deny her feelings had changed since they'd gone to the mission district YMCA. As Garth coached those boys she'd seen a side of him she didn't know. If only she hadn't agreed to go to his parents' house. If only . . .

"Kris? We're in here!"

Mandie's voice told her she'd walked right past the mini-conference room.

"And where are you today? Still down at the Y?" Mandie teased, sitting beside Hank on a navy blue couch.

"Guess I am in a fog," Kris admitted. "Connie, it's good to see you."

"Hi, Kris, " the social worker replied. "How's that baby girl?"

Kris relaxed. At least on this topic she was on firm ground. Kyung's progress since surgery had been excellent.

"Four days post-op," she answered. "Off her respirator in one day and out of ICU the next. She'll start oral foods this morning. No more IV if she does well. Her progress is even better than we'd hoped for."

"And she's smiling up a storm," Mandie added. "She's a whole new child!"

"I'm glad to hear that." Connie O'Malley shifted her notebook on her lap. "I wanted to meet with the three of you for two reasons. First, Hank and Mandie's temporary foster care license has been granted. Everything's in place. I so enjoyed seeing your home yesterday."

"We were pretty nervous," Hank admitted. "Everything was all right?"

"That kind of thing makes everyone nervous. It was more than all right. Which brings me to the second reason I called us together." She smoothed the notebook's cover. "Last night I learned that there's a strong possibility Kyung may be available for adoption. How would you feel about that?"

Mandie gasped. Hank moved to the edge of the couch, his eyes riveted to Connie's. "You mean . . . real adoption?" he said carefully. "She'd be . . . our child?"

Once again Mandie's eyes turned almost black from excitement as she strained to hear the social worker's reply.

Chapter Fifteen

"Yes, really yours," Connie assured them. "But it would take time. And there are some things you need to understand. We know Kyung is Korean-American, but her country can't find any records of her birth. If she returns to Korea, it isn't likely that she would be adopted. She'd almost certainly grow up in the orphanage." Connie paused, as if searching for words.

"Technically," she continued, "she's known as an alien orphan. Her country has been most positive about her remaining here. But I need to tell you this could cost several thousand dollars before it's over."

"I didn't really want to restore that '63 Chevy anyhow," Hank laughed. "How long would it take, Mrs. O'Malley, before she'd be ours?"

"Well, first you'd need a more detailed home study and a state-approved case worker. The former is no problem, and I qualify as the latter." Connie leaned forward. "Her birth country must grant her a visa, the complete home study has to be approved, references checked, and any other immigration requirements met." She smiled. "The good part is you'd have her living with you during all this, first as foster parents, and later as adoptive parents."

"Oh, Hank!" Mandie breathed.

"Then she'd be with you for six months, more or less, before formal adoption proceedings."

"And then what?" Mandie pressed.

"Ninety-nine percent of the time, if it gets that far the adoption goes through. As I said, it takes about six months. After a short court appearance she'd become legally yours."

"That's it?" Hank asked.

"Basically, yes. I would never have suggested it if I didn't feel there's a strong chance of successful adoption. I know how much this means to you."

Mandie's dark eyes turned to Hank, then back to Connie. "We haven't let ourselves think of adoption even for a second," she said emphatically. "How did it come about?"

"Last night I talked to the director of Operation Search, and he brought it up. He was most optimistic."

"What about U.S. citizenship?" Hank wanted to know.

"She'd live with you as the adopting parents for two years. After a court appearance she'd become a lawful, permanent resident of the United States."

The look on Hank's face made Kris turn her head away. She heard Mandie whisper, "Oh, Hank, God's answered our prayers."

"He's done that, all right," Hank whispered back. Then he cleared his throat. "Mrs. O'Malley, what can I say except . . . thanks." Hank's mouth quivered, and he paused for several seconds. "Whatever it takes, we'll do. Whatever it takes."

Connie O'Malley reached for her jacket. "I know that, Hank. This is one family God definitely put together. I'll start adoption proceedings right away, and be in touch in a few days." She extended her hands in a warm goodbye.

As soon as she left, Kris grabbed both of her friends in an enormous, joyful hug.

"SURE YOU CAN GET along with only four of you?"

"Karen, you'll only be gone an hour," Kris laughed. 'I've got plenty of help. As many of your crew as possible should hear Dr. Sydney's lecture. He's outstanding." Kris waved the evening shift nurse manager away.

Working an extra hour was no problem. She'd planned to catch up on paperwork tonight anyhow, and she'd still be home in time for Mandie's call. It made her happy just thinking of Hank and Mandie's undisguised excitement as they took off for a celebration dinner and shopping trip for baby clothes.

Chapter Fifteen

"Anything special you'd like me to do before dinner trays arrive, Kris?"

Sylvia Ivers waited beside the nurses' station entrance. Sylvia had been a mainstay on the peds evening shift for years.

Kris checked the time, glad for the offer. "Thanks, Sylvia. We should probably look in on patients. You take the left side, I'll take the right. Meet you back here in ten minutes."

Kris slipped a stethoscope around her neck and a fresh memo pad in her pocket, then started down the hall. The floor hummed with the lazy, peaceful sounds of late afternoon. She was glad that despite the high case load, they didn't have many critically ill children. She entered a room occupied by two pre-teenagers.

"Hi, Roger," she smiled. "How's the leg?"

"It's cool. Might spring this place tomorrow." The husky boy's casual words failed to conceal the hope in his eyes.

"You just might do that, Rog, if you do everything Dr. Endicott says." She checked the second bed and made note of the patient's pallor and rigid body position. "Hey, Ed, that incision acting up again?"

He grimaced.

"Try to relax, and I'll send something for pain right away." Kris jotted a note on her tablet and returned to the hall.

A spacious linen storage area separated the older patients' section from one of several four-bed units reserved for babies and toddlers. She walked to the middle of the room, sensing something wrong. Her eyes bounded from one patient to the next, then stopped. The bed next to the window—Kyung's bed—was much too quiet. Kris looked again, closer this time. Kyung Lee wasn't breathing.

Kris acted on instinct, with precision and economy of every move. As she kicked the crib release she studied the deathly still baby, taking lightning inventory of her symptoms. An ominous dusky hue overshadowed Kyung's beautiful olive skin. Her eyes were half-shut, her mouth open. A faint stream of milk trickled from one corner, down her cheek, and disappeared behind a tiny ear. Kris probed the baby's neck, searching for a carotid pulse. None. She jerked the stethoscope into place, straining for a heartbeat. Feeble, but present.

"Kyung?" Kris lifted her, bracing the slender neck and rolling head with one hand. "Hey, sweetheart. Hey, little one." *Please, God, not Hank and Mandie's baby!*

The baby's arms and legs dangled unnaturally on either side of Kris's right arm as more milk trickled out of her half-open mouth.

At that moment Kris realized what had happened and stretched toward the wall to jerk on the suction machine switch. Kyung had been given her first bottle this afternoon, after four days of intravenous feeding. Somehow she must have turned onto her back and aspirated formula into her lungs. How far had it gone? How long had she been like this? Had her newly repaired heart been damaged?

Kris lowered Kyung to the bed and squeezed her cheeks together, forcing her mouth open as she gently inserted the tiny tip of the plastic cannula, urging it further and further toward the back of the throat and down the trachea. At last it stabilized, letting Kris know she had reached the bronchial tubes. She stretched sideways just long enough to flip on the vital intercom, then in one motion turned back to Kyung, releasing the suction as a steady stream of milk flowed through the transparent tube.

"Desk, Miss Ivers speaking," the intercom barked.

"Sylvia?" Kris called over the noise of the suction. In the next crib nine-month-old Pablo wailed loudly, frightened by the sudden noise. "Sylvia . . . Kris. In the babies' unit. Emergency. Is Dr. Endicott there?"

Chapter Fifteen

"Yes. Right down, Kris. Hold on!"

Instead, it seemed an eternity since she'd found Kyung of a minute and a half. No more milk flowed through the catheter, but she continued to probe. Even a drop remaining in the lungs could be lethal. Then she felt Kyung's head move and a second later roll the other way. A surge of joy coursed through her as she realized Kyung was trying to get away from the catheter.

"Kris, what—?"

Garth stood close by, but she dared not turn away. She sensed Sylvia beside her and moved to the right, allowing the other nurse to control Kyung's now-flailing arms.

"Formula aspiration. Maybe two minutes ago."

"Any pulse?" Garth slipped a stethoscope in place.

"None when I found her—just a faint heartbeat. I pray that heart can take it."

As she spoke Kyung screamed, vigorous and protesting, in concert with the howling Pablo. Kris laughed, happier than she'd have believed possible.

"Come on, baby, you tell 'em!" she coaxed.

Garth finished his examination and slowly pulled the stethoscope from his ears. "You can stop, Kris. She'll be fine."

Gently and with great care Kris withdrew the catheter as Kyung yelled with new vigor, free of the hated object. Pablo's terrified cries increased.

Kris grinned at Garth as she lifted Kyung from the crib.

"You tell 'em, sweetie," she murmured, thankful for every breath the baby took. "Come on . . . let's hear some more."

"Hey, little guy," Sylvia said, hurrying to Pablo's crib. "Nothing's that bad. Come on now." She reached the edge of the crib and lifted out the dark-skinned baby boy.

Soon the room was silent once again. Kris continued to hold Kyung, stroking her soft, small back as she rocked from one foot to the other. She looked up at Garth, her eyes clouded with the reality of what almost happened.

"Mandie and Hank are out buying baby clothes this very minute. If anything happened to her, I'd—"

"But it didn't, Kris," Garth said quickly, his words resonant with admiration. "Your fast work saved her life. No doubt of it. Even a couple minutes longer and we might have lost her. The heart's healing well, but that kind of strain. . . ."

Kris cradled Kyung on her shoulder. "I don't understand. She'd done fine with her water all day, so we gave her the first formula around one-thirty this afternoon. She seemed to tolerate it so well."

"They usually do. She may have taken too much or eaten too fast. It's hard to say. Let's cut her to no more than two ounces per feeding, and keep a nurse with her constantly for a while. This probably won't happen again, but we can't take any chances."

Kris looked over at Sylvia, holding a sleeping Pablo in the rocking chair at the other end of the room. "Sylvia, could you stay in here until the others get back, please? It shouldn't be long."

"Sure. I think Pablo would appreciate that."

Kris carefully settled the now-sleeping Kyung on her side with a rolled blanket braced against her back. As she and Garth left the room, the clock read a quarter past four.

"Garth, Mandie and Hank are calling me tonight. Do you think I should tell them about this, or wait until tomorrow?"

"I think they ought to know tonight. Why don't you let me call them?"

"I'd appreciate that. They'll be home around nine."

"Good. I'll call them. There are a few things they should know. That baby's alive because of you, Kris." Garth's voice was tender. "Do you have any idea how special you are?"

She looked down, unsure of herself for the first time since she had walked into Kyung's room.

16

KRIS FELT AWFUL. Garth's mother had probably gone to a lot of trouble fixing a special dinner. Too bad she wouldn't be able to eat a bite.

Her heart pounded, her hands were clammy, and every time she tried to smile her face quivered like half-set Jello. Why had she ever let herself get talked into this? She stole a sideways look at Garth, so relaxed as he negotiated the Saturday afternoon traffic. Did he have the most remote concept of what this invitation was putting her through?

As if aware of her thoughts, he covered her clenched hands with his. "You look beautiful, Kris. And it's going to be fun. You'll see."

She tried to think of something to say, other than how scared she was. "Exactly where is your parents' home? I know we're driving towards the ocean, but after that I'm lost."

"It's in an area called Seacliff, in northwest San Francisco. They've lived there for years, and sometimes I wonder why they stay. It's right on the ocean, so it's foggy a lot of the time.

But they love it." He glanced over his shoulder and pulled into the right lane. He looked wonderful in a blue-brown cotton sweater pulled over an open-necked shirt.

"Right now I think the fog's winning." All day she'd watched the familiar gray band of clouds play hide-and-seek with the city. From time to time it receded, allowing narrow shafts of sunlight to tease the buildings with warmth. But always the fog crept back.

She smoothed her cotton madras skirt. Her bright coral sweater over a coral-pink linen blouse looked happy on this gray day, blending with the skirt's blue and coral stripes. Tiny pearl earrings were just enough jewelry, barely visible under her tied-back hair. It never hurt to look cheerful, especially considering the drippy weather, and the warmth of the sweater felt good.

Garth made another right turn, and the abrupt closeness of the vast, gray-blue ocean startled her.

"Almost there," he remarked.

She knew he meant to reassure her, but her stomach turned over. The car slowed down and after several blocks entered an area of the most beautiful homes Kris had ever seen. Most were stone or brick, and some were sprawling, newer homes built from handsome weathered wood. As they drove the fog seemed to thicken.

"The ocean's only about a mile away," he explained, as though reading her mind.

Once in fifth grade, the teacher had asked her to get a library book from an absent pupil's desk. Bending to retrieve it, she'd noticed the student's open box of prized trading cards inside the desk. They were much better than her own collection, and on impulse she'd slipped a dozen into her pocket.

When the girl returned two days later she'd recognized her cards among Kris's, and accused Kris of stealing them. After two days of tears and vehement denials, she finally confessed the truth to Grandma, who had personally walked Kris to the teacher's home to set things right. All the way there Kris hoped something would happen, anything to prevent their arrival.

In a few minutes Garth's car would pull into a driveway and she'd be face-to-face with his parents. She felt exactly as she had that long-ago day at school, and wished with all her heart they'd never arrive.

"See that brick house at the end of the street? That's it." He turned into a curving driveway edged with blue lobelia and yellow marigolds, and shut off the motor. A two-story house loomed above them, guarded by an ancient sycamore tree.

Kris felt paralyzed as Garth circled the car. They walked in silence up the curved, old brick path to the house. On either side of the wide brick porch hung several white fuchsias, responding with luxuriant growth to the damp, foggy air. They stopped in front of two carved wooden doors, and Kris clutched her purse with both hands to hide their trembling. Garth turned the massive brass knob and flung open the doors.

"Anybody home?" he yelled. He touched her elbow and she stepped inside the spacious entrance hall. To their left a low pewter bowl of creamy, fragrant gardenias stood on a gleaming mahogany table. Usually she loved them, but today their sweet perfume made her sick.

A woman came hurrying toward the door, wearing fluffy maroon bedroom slippers and a huge pink apron edged with white rick-rack. The voluminous pink creation nearly obscured a simple navy blue linen dress. Her thick hair was salt-and-pepper gray, the style uncertain.

"Garth! Hello, son."

"Mom, this is Kris. Kris, meet my mother, Mrs. Endicott." Garth's voice was warm as he introduced the two of them.

She nodded somberly, afraid if she smiled her twitching

face muscles would betray her. If Garth hadn't identified his mother, Kris would have thought she was meeting the family cook.

Standing on a thick Oriental rug and surrounded by exquisite antiques, Mrs. Endicott was the exact opposite of what Kris had expected. She wore almost no makeup, and her dark eyes flashed Kris a smile of welcoming friendship.

"I—I'm so glad to meet you, Mrs. Endicott," she stammered, feeling faint from anxiety and the pungent gardenias.

"Kris, I'm so glad to meet you at last. How about a cup of coffee before we meet the rest of this bunch?" She gestured vaguely toward the sound of voices from another part of the house. "If you're like I am, the fun's in the knowing, not the meeting! Garth, we'll see you later. We're going to the kitchen."

Kris looked back at him wildly, but as Mrs. Endicott grabbed her hand there was nothing to do but follow the pink apron through the restful living room. As she walked, Kris felt a tiny fraction of her panic subside. Funny how much it helped to do something.

She glanced briefly at the large picture windows lining the far end of the room, then beyond them to a long wooden deck. Below it a small, bright green lawn curved its way over a sloping hill, edged on three sides with roses, marigolds, zinnias, evergreen shrubs, and varieties of flowers Kris had never seen. The lawn ended at the base of a broad flagstone wall. Less than two blocks past the wall surged the restless ocean. Kris stopped, spellbound by the scene.

"I love the ocean, don't you, Kris?"

Kris looked over, embarrassed "Oh, Mrs. Endicott. It's all so beautiful."

"I'm glad you like it. We've lived here for over thirty years, and I'm not used to it yet. Now, why don't you come on into the kitchen? The view's exactly the same there."

Kris followed her through a swinging wooden door into the large kitchen. Blue and white tiles with a Dutch design lined the counters and the walls behind them. Half-curtains of the identical pattern covered a window facing the driveway. On the ocean side of the room an old wooden table and eight chairs invited people to enjoy the spectacular view she'd seen from the living room.

"What a wonderful room!" Kris exclaimed, at home in the kitchen. "I'd never want to leave it!" Her face reacted normally now and she no longer felt sick. Unable to eat breakfast, she suddenly felt more than a passing interest in the aromas of almond-blend coffee, roast turkey, and fresh rolls. A warm feeling of safety replaced the anguish of only minutes ago.

Mrs. Endicott chuckled as the door swung shut behind them. "I manage to leave it often enough," she said, walking to the sink. "But I enjoy cooking. Especially when the children come. Here, Kris. I baked some pies yesterday. Just put them on the table by the window."

Kris carefully moved the golden pies one by one, drinking in the ocean view each time she placed another on the table. How, she wondered, could she have thought of this day as gloomy?

"Thanks. Now why don't you pour yourself a cup of coffee? Then we can talk while you cut these things into the salad bowl." Mrs. Endicott moved a pile of celery stalks onto a chopping board and placed a small knife beside them. "There's something about me that son of ours may not have told you. Did you know I'm a nurse, too?" Mrs. Endicott stirred a large pan of gravy and laughed. "I'd better change that. I used to be a nurse."

Kris liked the sound of her laughter. It was loud and real and something about it made her want to smile.

"No, I didn't realize that," she answered, hoping she

was slicing the celery thin enough. "What field were you in?"

"Well, I enjoyed obstetrics. Guess it was contagious, because before long I was a patient there instead of part of the staff." She covered the rolls with a towel as she talked. "I made three visits, and pretty soon all the nursing I had time for was right here at home."

"Nothing's more important than that." Kris smiled at Mrs. Endicott, feeling more relaxed by the minute. "Is this celery all right?"

"Is what all right?"

Kris looked up from the chopping block in time to see Garth duck his head as he walked through the swinging door. He was followed by a tall, distinguished looking man with silvery hair and blue-green eyes.

"Dad, this is Kris Carothers. Kris, meet my father." Garth grabbed a stalk of celery as he spoke.

Kris wiped her hand on a tea towel and extended it to Garth's father.

"So this is Kris," Dr. Endicott said, his tone as friendly and comfortable as his wife's.

"Dr. Endicott," she smiled, "I'm so glad to meet you." The past twenty minutes had swept away every trace of panic. She sensed that no matter what she did wrong, it wouldn't matter to Garth's family. This day might turn out just fine . . . so long as nobody asked too many questions about her own family.

"Mom, can you spare Kris for a while?" Garth asked. "I want her to meet Bruce and David and the others. I'll bring her back soon."

"Go on," his mother told him. "And make sure she meets the children!"

Garth's brothers, their wives, and children were scattered through the house. Some were on the deck, protected from the damp fog by a geranium-filled solarium. They found the older children in the paneled den on the far side of the living room, working a puzzle as they stretched out on a large Indian rug.

Garth led her from one person to another, and—to her amazement—Kris found herself enjoying their company. Later the two of them walked outside the flagstone wall to listen to the pounding surf. Kris wondered if maybe Grandma had been wrong when she said the doctor's children in Willows had their own friends and Kris wasn't one of them. . . .

Half an hour later everyone helped Mrs. Endicott carry serving dishes of roast turkey, gravy, mashed potatoes, peas, green salad, rolls, and fresh cranberry-orange relish to the table. On each trip Kris tried to study something different in the handsome dining room.

The table was well over ten feet long, covered with a woven, off-white tablecloth. In its center fresh yellow roses overflowed a large crystal bowl. And like a house trademark the restless ocean, barely visible through the fog, dominated the room.

When everyone had gathered together around the table, Dr. Endicott cleared his throat. "I'll offer thanks," he said simply.

His words were a memorized blessing Kris had heard before, different from the spontaneous prayer she was used to, but the measured and careful way he prayed told Kris that Garth's handsome father was a man of faith.

Their dinner was unhurried and calm. Conversation centered on medicine, the progress of the Giants, and the senior Endicotts' upcoming annual exodus to Santa Barbara for some warm sun. And Mrs. Endicott's peach, cherry, and Dutch apple pies tasted even better than they looked.

Later, standing with Garth by the open front doors, Kris actually wished they didn't have to leave. Behind her the fog, now almost a misty rain, swirled around the hanging fuchsias, illuminated by two brass porch lights. David, Bruce, and their families had left as soon as dessert was over, anxious to get their children home to bed.

Now Dr. and Mrs. Endicott stood in the entry hall to say goodnight to Kris and their youngest son.

"Garth, you bring her back soon, won't you?"

"I promise, Mom," he said with a laugh. "Call you tomorrow."

"I can't tell you how much I've enjoyed this," Kris told them warmly, offering her hand to Dr. Endicott, who clasped it between both of his.

"Good having you, Kris. Come back soon," he urged her.

As Mrs. Endicott stretched out her hand, their eyes met, and Kris found herself wrapped in a spontaneous hug.

"You come back and I'll teach you to make pie crust!"

Kris was quiet as Garth drove slowly through the fog. He'd been right. The evening had been fun—and unlike anything she'd expected.

"Garth," she said at last, "you have one of the nicest families I've ever met."

He dimmed his lights for a passing car. "They're tops, Mom and Dad. I had a feeling you'd like 'em."

That's an understatement, Kris thought. There was no question that the Endicott and Carothers families were from entirely different worlds. The Endicotts knew about all kinds of things she'd never heard of. They'd traveled to places she couldn't pronounce. Yet she'd never felt so accepted in her life.

She rested her head on the back of the seat, watching the fog swirl around the glowing street lights.

How strange life was. A week ago she'd gone out to dinner with Todd after looking forward to it for days, and been so disappointed. She'd dreaded tonight . . . yet enjoyed it more than she could have imagined.

Chapter Sixteen

As Garth pulled up to the curb, the wet cement steps of Kris's apartment glistened in the dampness like tiny diamonds. She wished somehow they could make the night's magic last just a little longer.

"Would you like some hot chocolate?"

"Sounds great. It's late June, but this sure is a hot chocolate night."

Kris smiled happily as they hurried up the steps. She unlocked the apartment and switched on the lamp near the bookcase.

"I found a pan. Shall I heat the milk?" Garth called from the kitchen.

Kris laughed. "Now that I've seen your mother in action I realize you probably know a lot more about cooking than I do." She walked into the kitchen and lifted two mugs from the cupboard.

"Mom was in her element tonight. She loves cooking for all of us," Garth said. "Family is one of the most important things in her life."

"It shows." Kris lifted out a can of cocoa mix from another cupboard. "I was raised that way too, but the emphasis was a lot different."

"How's that?"

"Well, family was the most important thing to us, too, but . . . well . . . I guess I ended up feeling it was us against the world. Grandma didn't believe in getting too close to other people."

"And she brought you up that way?"

Garth carefully poured the steaming milk into the mugs as Kris stirred the cocoa mix to a rich, dark brown.

"Yes," Kris answered, on guard for the first time in hours. The contrast between their families was unbearable.

"Well, all I know is your grandma must be a wonderful person."

"She is," Kris laughed, grateful to him for saying it, "but

how could you know that?"

"Because . . . she raised you."

Their eyes held briefly until Kris picked up her mug and pointed to the living room. "Why don't we sit in there for once?"

They settled themselves on the wicker couch and sat together in the dim light in an easy silence. "And how do you feel about family, Kris?" Garth asked after several minutes.

"I'm pretty old-fashioned. Marriage, children, I hope." She stopped, glad he couldn't see her face. She searched her mind frantically for another subject.

"One man, one woman?" he continued.

She nodded weakly, then had a burst of inspiration. "Speaking of family," she said brightly, "I wonder how Mandie and Hank are coming along, getting ready for Kyung's arrival?"

"I'm sure they're managing just fine," Garth answered. His tone suggested that this was enough discussion about the Dixons. He placed his empty mug on the floor to the right of the couch. Then he took Kris's mug and placed it carefully beside his, still saying nothing. As he straightened up he moved closer, slipping his left arm behind her shoulders.

"Kris," he whispered. He hadn't been this near to her in weeks, not since—

His hand stroked her cheek, strong and warm against her skin. He moved it back, working his fingers through her hair as he pulled her to him. "Kris," he murmured gruffly, "you mean more to me than I can ever put into words."

Then his gentle mouth was on hers, and his arms tightened around her with an unfamiliar urgency. A shimmering warmth surfaced in her heart and mind, unlike anything she'd felt before. This time she didn't struggle, but instinctively slipped her arms around him. She felt the muscles of his back under her hands, the rough warmth of his head as he kissed her again and again.

He slowly pulled away and Kris blinked in the semi-darkness, unable to sift through her exploding emotions. Garth's eyes probed hers, his hand tracing the outline of her chin and lips.

"Kris, I . . . it's late. Will you be in church tomorrow?" He softly kissed her forehead.

"Yes," she whispered, not trusting herself to say more. They stood together and walked as one through the quiet living room.

She closed the door and leaned against it, listening until she could no longer hear his footsteps. She stared long at the wicker couch, reliving every detail of his kiss.

Until tonight she'd insisted they be only friends, convinced it could never become more. He'd tried to do as she'd asked, of that she was certain. But now. . . . She shook her head, joyously happy and confused all at once. Tonight she'd felt something new, a tenderness and desire that she sensed went far, far beyond friendship.

"Oh, Garth," she whispered, and smiled, finding new delight in the sound of his name. She closed her eyes.

Please stop me now, Lord . . . stop me now if this is not Your will.

17

KRIS LEANED BACK IN HER CHAIR and stretched. Four times she'd added up the column of admission figures, with four different results. All week long, no matter how hard she had tried to focus on something else, she'd ended up thinking of Garth. He'd called every night this week and the more she listened to his voice, the worse it got.

His eyes smiled back at her from the lined page of admission statistics. His strong fingers traced the outline of her lips. His voice echoed in the hall, when she knew for a fact he was downstairs in an all-morning meeting.

She exited from the computer file and looked over at Carmen. "Think I'll see how the Dixons are coming. Be right back." Maybe a change of scene would help.

"Hey, Dixons—about ready to go?" she called from the doorway of Kyung's room. At the sound of her voice, Pablo looked up and gripped his crib bars, pulling himself to a precarious stand.

"Hi, Kris," Mandie answered. She and Hank stood on either

side of Kyung's crib. "C'mon in."

"For a Friday, things are pretty quiet around here," Kris said, rumpling Pablo's thick black hair. "Thought I'd see how you're coming."

"We'd be doing better if this little girl would hold still," Mandie replied. "All right, Kris. What do you think?" Held high in the air, Kyung drooled and kicked in a red, white, and blue terry cloth jogging suit.

"She's adorable," Kris exclaimed, affectionately smoothing Kyung's dark hair.

"Somehow it seemed right," Hank explained. "She's on the way to her first real home, and in a brand-new country. Red, white, and blue says it all." He held out his arms and Mandie handed him the excited baby.

"Without you, Kris, this day wouldn't have come. Kyung might have had a perfect heart, but we'd have lost her all the same." Mandie's voice trembled. "We'll never be able to thank you."

"Mandie," Kris said kindly, "that's our job, remember? You'd have done the same thing. And seeing you and Hank with your little daughter is all the thanks I'll ever need."

"Our daughter," Mandie repeated. "Our daughter. I can't believe it."

"Okay, ladies," Hank interrupted. "Ready to go?"

After a final inspection the new family marched down the hall, Mandie carrying a bright-eyed Kyung resplendent in her new suit, Hank beside her with a tiny yellow suitcase, Kris next to him. As they approached the nurses' station, Connie O'Malley, Leona Steelman, and Ron Talbot stepped forward. Across the hall, almost hidden by her cleaning cart, waited Sophie.

"We came to say goodbye," Mr. Talbot said, shaking Hank's hand. "I feel as if I've had a personal role in this!"

"You have, Mr. Talbot. And thanks for everything," Mandie answered. "I promise we'll bring Kyung back to see you!"

"Being a social worker has many advantages," Connie O'Malley added, "and one of them will be visiting this little girl often." She hugged Mandie. "God bless you, dear."

Sophie left her cart and handed a small, tissue-wrapped package to Mandie. "You can open it now."

Mandie unwrapped two round bibs, one embroidered with kittens and the other with baby birds, both edged in a graceful feather stitch. "Sophie, they're beautiful! And you made them, didn't you?"

"Yes. I set the altar cloths aside for awhile. I'll miss cleaning this little girl's room each day." She caressed Kyung's cheek with a calloused hand.

"She'll come back to see you . . . wearing her best bib!"

"It's good to see a maneuver like this one end happily," said Leona Steelman, a faint smile skirting her face as she patted Kyung.

Several of the floor nurses joined the small group waving good-bye until the elevator doors closed between them and they were on their way. Kris accompanied her friends out to the car, where it took the three of them ten minutes to figure out how to settle Kyung into her new car seat. At last they were ready.

Kris felt a lump in her throat as the car and its precious cargo disappeared. Without question Mandie needed her requested month's leave of absence, but Kris missed her already. How mysterious were God's ways, how far beyond her understanding. Less than two months ago Hank and Mandie had all but given up hope for a family. Today they were beginning a new life with a baby only the Lord Himself could have sent.

Deep in thought and shivering in the cool June air, Kris returned to the comfortable lobby. As she started across the room to the elevator, she sensed someone watching her. In the far corner Dr. Burack slumped in an overstuffed chair, a nearby table lamp illuminating his small, penetrating eyes.

Chapter Seventeen

The lobby clock read eleven-thirty.

What was Fred Burack doing down here, alone, at this hour of the morning? Kris turned her head in the other direction, still feeling his arrogant gaze after the elevator doors closed behind her. With a silent prayer she forced him from her mind. She'd get back to work and forget about Dr. Burack and even about Garth long enough to finish the census tally.

KRIS CLOSED THE FILE AND CHECKED her watch. One-fifteen, time to stop for lunch. At least she'd completed the tally, if little else.

"I'm going to the lounge for a few minutes, Carmen, then up to the Roof."

"Well, it's about time," she teased. "Good thing the weekend's coming, isn't it?"

Kris laughed, wondering how much Carmen had already figured out. She was glad to find the nurses' lounge empty and walked to the window. One of her favorite views, it afforded a jewel-like perspective of the city as it sloped from the towering hospital to the ocean.

She rubbed her arms, relieving the stiffness from the hours at her desk. Too bad administrative nursing involved so much paperwork—caring for people was what nursing was all about.

She smiled, remembering Mrs. Endicott's tale of how she'd left the profession. Three little boys and she'd said good-bye to nursing. And the last of those little boys had been Garth. Dr. Garth Endicott.

How her world had changed since last Saturday. Even before that, she conceded, looking down at the roofs below.

She'd never felt this way before, not even about Todd. Maybe there was a way to bridge their worlds after all . . . her poverty and his wealth . . . her plainness and his splendor.

Kris sat down on the edge of the couch. It was good to be alone, good to have the luxury of uninterrupted thought. All day long the memory of Garth's kiss had waited, suspended near the edges of her mind. It lingered there, held in the wings of conscious thought until she allowed it center stage once more. She closed her eyes and dropped her head in her hands.

This had to stop. But she knew it wouldn't end until she saw him again.

She reapplied lip gloss, walked to the elevator and pushed the twelfth floor button. There were still twenty minutes of her lunch break. A small salad would hit the spot. She wished she'd brought something to read, since at this late hour nobody would be in the dining room.

A quick glance around the Roof Restaurant confirmed her hunch. Only a handful of people on afternoon coffee breaks were scattered around the large room. She started toward the counter and stopped, her eyes pinned to a small table in the farthest corner. There a man with familiar broad shoulders sat engrossed in conversation with a remarkably beautiful woman.

Even from this distance she recognized Garth and Sybil, oblivious to everyone but themselves. He looked relaxed in his tweed sport jacket; she was poised, laughing, never taking her eyes from his face. They looked perfect together.

Kris raised a tight fist to her mouth and backed into the still-open elevator. She punched the basement button and slumped against the wall, her eyes closed. The elevator stopped at the sixth floor, and Nineveh walked in carrying two bouquets.

"Miss Carothers, I'm glad to see—" he tipped his head at her—"you in the elevator ridin' with me."

"Y—yes," Kris stammered, not looking up.

"I think there's something I don't know." He cleared his throat.

Chapter Seventeen

"I'm sorry," Kris mumbled, fighting back an almost uncontrollable need to cry.

"—And it's high time that I just go." They reached the main floor and Nineveh backed out, blinking nervously.

As the elevator doors closed behind him, Kris's eyes flooded with tears she could no longer hold back. She wanted only one thing—to be alone. The brief descent quickly ended and she stepped into the wide basement hall. Several doors down, the familiar prayer chapel sign caught her eyes. She rushed toward it and pushed open the door.

Kris sank into a chair at one end of the empty room, again pressing a fist against her mouth. She lowered her head to her arms, out of control and helpless to stop.

After many minutes the sobs grew further apart and she lifted her head. As if in slow motion she brushed both hands over her tear-soaked cheeks and reddened eyes. She had to get hold of herself. She leaned back in the chair and took a long, deep breath and gradually released it. What a fool she'd been! And it really wasn't Garth's fault. . . .

Fresh tears welled up at the thought of his name, and she struggled again for control. She searched her pockets for a tissue, staring through wet lashes across the tiny room. Why had she ever let herself care so much?

She'd always known Garth wasn't her kind. She'd tried for so long to resist him, afraid even to dream he could care for someone like her. And probably he found that resistance appealing.

"Stay with your own kind," Grandma had warned her a hundred times. She should have listened.

After last Saturday night, Garth must have sensed the hunt was over and turned to more interesting fields. Sybil. She could never compete with Sybil's inborn style and assurance. Of course Sybil was the kind of woman Garth Endicott would want. She'd been born into his kind of world, spoke his language by instinct, understood him in ways Kris could never hope to.

But Garth. . . . She took another long, slow breath. All those words. Had they meant nothing? Were they just one more nice story?

She poked a finger through the damp tissue. What a little fool she'd been to think things could ever change between them!

Her eyes circled the room and stopped at the simple wooden cross on the front table. She stared at it for several minutes, remembering. Just the other night she'd asked the Lord to show her if what she was beginning to feel for Garth wasn't His will. She trembled, realizing that was exactly what He was doing. God was closing the door on those feelings once and for all.

She wanted to obey Him . . . but the obedience pierced her heart like a knife.

Kris stood up, lightheaded and feeling drained from emotion and lack of food. She'd do something about her appearance, drink some orange juice, and get back to the Pavilion. Then she'd work for hours . . . work until she was too exhausted to feel anything.

18

*K*RIS RESTED HER ACHING HEAD on the edge of the utility room window and thought back to another evening two short months ago. She and Garth had worked late, then walked the three blocks to her apartment in an early summer twilight's violet haze. It was only the second time he'd been there, and they'd talked about her faith, made plans for him to visit her church. . . .

"Kris, don't tell me you're still here? It's nine-thirty!" Doreen McFarlane balanced a medicine tray in one hand and pointed at the clock with the other.

"Is it really that late? I had a lot to finish up."

"Are you okay, Kris? You don't look like yourself tonight."

"I'm fine. But guess I should get going." The dark circles under her eyes told the story of this horrible day. She'd been on her feet more than fourteen hours now. But maybe she'd be able to sleep tonight, and for a few hours, forget.

"Then go—good-bye!" Doreen waved, resuming her journey down the darkened hall.

Five minutes later Kris stepped from the deserted lobby into the moonless night. July was less than two weeks away, but the air felt cool and she wished she'd worn a sweater. At least she only had three blocks to go.

She hurried past the doctors' parking lot, unable to resist a quick check of the few cars still there. Garth's wasn't among them. He'd been on and off the floor all day, mostly off. And she was sure she knew why.

She'd almost passed the parking area when a car door slammed at the far end. Instinctively she turned in the sound's direction and saw that it came from a new blue Cadillac. Dr. Burack, trim in a short-sleeved white shirt and gray slacks, walked toward her.

"Well, if it isn't Miss Carothers—and all alone." He stepped over the heavy chain enclosing the lot, disregarding her silence. "It's late for a nice little girl to be all alone by herself."

Her heart beat faster. His voice sounded different tonight, his speech more intense. As usual he avoided her eyes. She walked faster, Dr. Burack in lockstep beside her.

The light on the corner turned red. Kris waited for it to change, paralyzed by a growing fear. His arm slid around her waist, and she stiffened. Why had she gone out alone like this? Why hadn't she been more careful? At last the light changed to green, and she hurried across the street. They were halfway into the next block before he spoke again.

"Miss Carothers, I have a charming idea. Let me buy you a drink. It'll help us both relax. I know a little spot down the hill we can go to."

The idea was revolting, but for a change he sounded pleasant. She hurried her steps toward the next street light, anxious to reach a lighted area.

"No, thanks. I don't have time right now. I need to—" She caught herself. If she admitted she was going home, he'd know she was there by herself.

Chapter Eighteen

"No time for a drink, then?" His words were clipped. He looked up and down the street, suddenly agitated, his head jerking from one side to the other. "Those were my mother's favorite words: 'I don't have time right now!' " His voice jumped in a cruel falsetto.

"No one ever has time for Freddie!" His arm tightened around her waist. "Well, tonight you're going to make time, beautiful lady. I need to hold you against me," he mumbled. "I can't wait any longer."

He pushed her sideways, forcing her off the sidewalk onto the grass in front of a brick building. It was Bill and Karen's apartment house. If only they'd be out on their patio. . . . If only she could get to them. . . .

Terrified, she regained her balance and ran. He matched her pace without effort, then gripped her upper arm with brutal strength. She cried out in sudden pain and twisted away, gasping as she stumbled ahead, hearing his laugh behind her.

He let her go for a few yards, watching her like a hawk with a mouse. Seconds later he caught up, clutching at her hips. She reeled around to face him, scratching wildly. Then he seized the front of her uniform and ripped it open to the waist.

He laughed loudly, slapping her hard across one cheek. She tasted blood and stumbled backwards, screaming for help. He lunged forward, then twisted both her arms behind her and shoved her into a narrow cement walkway between the brick apartment and the next.

"Freddie's got something all ready for you," he wheezed. With cruel force he pushed her back, groping for her mouth. His arms pinned her against the brick wall, and she bit one with all her strength.

He swore in pain, then grabbed her, ripping her underclothes open with savage strength.

"Little witch," he hissed, slapping her with the back of

his hand and hurling her to the ground. The cement scraped against her bare flesh. Then he was on top of her, fumbling with his belt, his breath like old cigarettes and rotten fruit.

Her own breath came in small, desperate gulps. Strange tiny lights danced where she knew there was only darkness. Then the black night closed in, and she remembered no more.

A BROAD RIBBON OF SUNLIGHT streamed through Kris's bedroom window. She rolled sideways to escape it and moaned from the pain of movement. The skin of her chest felt as if it were on fire. In her nightmare he was on top of her again, crushing her breath, pushing her skirt up with his hands. She screamed in terror.

"Kris, it's all right. It's over. It's all right!"

At the sound of Mandie's voice, Kris opened her eyes and recognized her friend's anguished face above her. She turned her head away, sobbing.

She felt the bed give as Mandie sat down on its edge, smoothing Kris's forehead and uncombed hair with long, soothing strokes.

"It's all over, Kris," she reassured her. "It's morning now. It's over." Her hand was cool, her touch the essence of kindness.

Kris took a slow, deep breath and then released it, studying her friend's face through a blur of tears. "Where is he?"

"Out of jail on bond, and the hospital's already suspended him. They're notifying the California Medical Association. There'll be a hearing. Apparently Dr. Burack's been involved with this kind of thing before—he's moved around a lot."

Kris took another deep breath and struggled to a sitting position, every joint stiff and aching, and painstakingly unfastened the buttons of her pajama top. Mandie moved back, and together they studied her throbbing chest, over half of it scraped raw in narrow, dark red strips. Their eyes met, sharing a pain beyond words.

One by one Kris redid the buttons, remembering the cement she'd skidded across after he hit her the second time. The dry burn on her delicate skin hurt more than she would have dreamed possible. She closed her eyes and sank into her pillow.

"How d'you feel?"

"Like I've been run over by a truck."

"You almost were," Mandie said quietly.

Kris tried to control her shaking voice. "I—I feel filthy, Mandie. That man . . ."

"You were not raped," Mandie said firmly. "Do you remember being checked out at the rape center last night?"

"Yes. I know . . . I know that technically I wasn't raped. But I feel raped, Mandie. I feel as if I'll never be really clean again!" She burst into tears and covered her face with her hands.

"Oh, my precious friend!" Mandie wrapped Kris in a gentle hug, her voice warm and protective. "They gave you something at the hospital last night, so you could sleep. You're feeling that on top of everything else."

"I remember, vaguely. What time is it, anyhow?"

"Nearly noon. At least you slept soundly, once you got the chance. It was past midnight when we got here—we came as soon as Bill and Karen called us."

"How long have you been up?"

"Since about eight. That's late for me these days. Kyung's an early bird." Mandie smiled.

"It meant so much to have you stay with me last night."

"Hank takes care of Kyung every bit as well as I do," Mandie replied. "Anyhow, I never could have left you. Listen, do you feel like moving into the kitchen? I could fix you a little breakfast."

Kris shook her head. "Thanks, but just the thought of food makes me sick. But maybe a cup of coffee." She pushed the covers back with her legs, then cautiously stood up and let Mandie help her into a robe. Still shaking, she walked slowly to the bathroom and brushed her teeth. When she finished she took a long look in the mirror.

Her upper lip was red and swollen, her face bruised along both cheekbones. Her eyes seemed to have sunk deep into her head. She groaned and looked away.

Mandie waited in the doorway. "It'll get better."

"I know. It's just that . . . rape is something that happens to other people. In some ways it seems like a bad dream."

"Before long it will be." Mandie circled Kris's shoulders with her arm and guided her into the kitchen, where she sank gratefully into a chair. Mandie poured her a mug of coffee.

Kris looked at the floor. "Thank goodness they took me to San Francisco General and not University." Her eyes swam with tears.

"It was a good choice," Mandie said kindly. She sat down across from her friend. "Kris, what was going on at work yesterday, anyway? Nineveh was so worried about you he called Doreen after he got home. She said you worked your own shift and then through most of hers."

Kris felt her whole body start to shake again. "I might as well tell you the whole thing, Mandie." She took another slow breath. "I've been a fool. Things between Garth and me had been getting, well, more and more special. Or so I thought. Maybe I lost touch with reality for a while. But then yesterday it hit me in the face."

"What did?"

"I saw Garth and Sybil up in the dining room." She wiped away more tears, wishing she could manage to stop crying. "Locked in a little world all their own. They looked so right together. They . . . fit. Garth and I don't." She pulled the potted geranium toward her and gently fingered a fuzzy leaf.

"So then what happened?"

"I think I sort of went crazy inside. I made up my mind I'd work till I dropped. I wanted to be so exhausted I'd sleep for hours and not have to think about him." She looked over at Mandie. "I knew from the start nothing could happen between us. But I was beginning to believe I'd been wrong, that he might actually—" Her voice broke.

She gingerly stood up and walked to the kitchen window. "Anyway, I worked from seven yesterday morning till nine-thirty last night. By the time I left I was almost in a daze—from being so tired, and from thinking about Garth and all. It was foolish, but I just walked out the hospital door and started home."

"Oh, Kris. Alone, and at that hour." There was gentle reproach in Mandie's voice.

"Yes. I know how stupid it was now, but then I didn't care." Kris closed her eyes and rubbed her head as if to forget. "When I walked past the doctors' parking lot, Dr. Burack got out of his car and started walking with me. I'm sure he'd been waiting. He wanted me to go out for a drink. When I said no, something inside him seemed to go wild."

Mandie flushed with anger. "All along you knew he was trouble, Kris, and the rest of us let you down. We never thought he'd do anything like this."

"He's always frightened me, but I never dreamed it would go this far, either. It happened so fast, Mandie, I couldn't even think. I didn't have a second to do anything, run anywhere. I've never been so terrified. "

Mandie reached across the table and squeezed Kris's hand. "At least you had the presence of mind to scream. As long as you keep an ex-cop for a neighbor, I guess you don't need to worry."

Kris started to smile, but her swollen lips burned with pain. "Bill's a good man. I just thank God he was home and heard me."

Mandie grimaced. "Evidently Fred took one look at Bill's revolver and cooled off like a glacier. And Karen said the police got there in under two minutes."

"I don't remember any of that. . . ."

"You fainted."

"I know. The second time he hit me, I—" She started to cry again.

"It'll take time to get over this, Kris, but you will. So many people care about you. Garth will want to see you as soon as you're ready. He'll be frantic when he hears."

Kris straightened in her chair. "I don't want to see Garth, except at work. I'll have to talk to him there, of course. But no more dates, or meetings, or any of that. And he mustn't know I saw him with Sybil. I just want to get out of his way."

"But, Kris—"

"I'll take a few days off, until I look better, then I'm going right back to work. Everybody'll know what happened, but I don't want to have to talk about it all the time. Especially not with Garth."

"But, Kris, don't you think talking about it will help you get over it?"

"I brought this on myself, Mandie. Dr. Burack is very sick, but I'm the one who allowed it to happen. In a way, I'm responsible."

"You're what?" Mandie's voice rose a full scale. "Kris, how could you even think that?"

"I'm too nice, too sweet, too everything." She shook her head angrily. "Sweet little Kris! If I hadn't wanted everyone to like me so much, it might never have happened."

"This doesn't make sense."

Kris pushed her hair back from her face with both

hands, bone-weary, longing for a shower and shampoo and a chance to feel clean again. "It makes more sense than I've made in years. Maybe I needed this to happen. To remind me once and for all what I am, where I came from." She slumped forward. "And after what happened last night, there's not the slightest chance Garth Endicott would get involved with me again. The sooner I face that, the better."

"I think you're wrong about Garth, Kris. Shouldn't you at least give him a chance to explain himself? Maybe what you saw wasn't what you thought."

"Mandie, it was a joke even to pretend he could ever care for me. And now. . . ."

The room was silent, flooded with midday sun and the sounds of the city at work. Mandie reached across the table and covered Kris's cold hand with hers.

"Give it time, Kris. Our God is in the miracle business. You told me that once, when I was desperate to hear it. Give it a little time. You don't have to decide everything today."

The power of her friend's faithfulness and love shattered Kris's taut control. "Bless you," she whispered, not even trying to brush away the tears.

19

TRUE TO HER WORD, Kris was back at work in less than a week. Her lip was almost normal, but her chest still burned if she moved too fast. Gradually food seemed interesting once again, and the terrifying nightmares grew further apart.

As her body steadily healed, the guilt gnawing from the inside grew worse. Each day the fact that Fred Burack had attacked her seemed less surprising. She'd been able to fool everyone but him. He'd seen right through her happy little Kris act. It was frightening to think how much he must have known about the part of her she'd tried so hard to hide. He'd recognized how unsure of herself she really was, had calculated her desperate need for acceptance.

Somehow, she decided, she'd provoked him, and that made her responsible for what finally happened. She'd always known she was different. Dr. Burack's violent attack only confirmed it. She was not worthy of Garth Endicott, and the hope that had burned brightly for a brief time flickered and died.

But there was one area where she did measure up, and that

was nursing. She threw herself into it, discovering that if she stayed busy enough she could almost forget her sadness and shame. But from time to time, she stopped working long enough to stare out a hospital window and fly back in time to the faded old wing chair in her childhood living room.

She remembered its musty smell, felt its smooth maroon and black fabric on her arms as she snuggled against it, pictured in her mind its threadbare, sagging seat. How she wished she could retreat to it now, and hide behind it the way she'd done as a little girl. From that safe place she could peek out at the world, and never be a bother to anyone.

Even the kindness of her friends failed to dilute the blame she heaped upon herself. Not Mandie's minestrone soup, not Carmen's Christmas burritos, not even Dr. and Mrs. Endicott's wicker basket of pink and white geraniums. And especially not Garth's nightly calls . . . or the yellow roses he'd had delivered to her apartment three times in twelve days. She responded to his kindness with cool politeness. The flowers were only a cover-up for pity.

He appeared to understand her need to move beyond what had happened to her, or perhaps Mandie had told him. Whatever the reason, he honored her wish, never moving too close as they reviewed lists of patients and their care. But from time to time she'd catch him looking at her with an unspoken question in his eyes. She always looked away, understanding that he, too, needed to move beyond what had happened between them.

ON THE THURSDAY AFTERNOON of her second week back, she made up her mind to take a long-overdue inventory of all medications on the Pavilion. She asked Carmen not to disturb her except for a genuine emergency. Soon she'd opened every cupboard in the treatment room, and calculator in hand started a meticulous tabulation from the top shelf to the bottom. She'd been at the absorbing task for over an hour when she heard a knock on the door.

"Come in, Carmen," she called, finishing the count on the top shelf.

"Hello, dear. I hope you don't mind a friendly interruption."

Kris climbed down from her stool to find herself face-to-face with Sybil. Today she was radiant in a soft blue summer dress, surrounded by a cloud of delicate perfume. Her bare arms were golden brown, her nails perfect, long and polished.

"How are you dear?" she asked with cloying concern. "I would have stopped by sooner, but all the family trotted off to Italy for a few weeks. You know what they say about all work and no play!" She laughed, spinning the bracelets on her slender wrist.

Kris knew. She leaned against a shelf and tried to smile. "That sounds nice," she remarked. "And I'm fine, thank you."

Sybil moved closer. "Was it just awful, dear . . . I mean . . .?"

Something inside Kris recoiled. "I'm trying to forget that now. Put it behind me."

Sybil smiled a wide, perfect smile. "Of course you are, dear . . . but you must feel so terribly alone now. I mean, considering what happened, and all. . . . "

Kris took a step forward, trembling with anger. "Sybil, I don't know what you came in here for, but this conversation is over."

Sybil took a step toward the door and then spun around, facing Kris. "You stay away from him, you hear?" The artificial sweetness in her voice had evaporated, and her beautiful eyes gleamed like green lasers. "Stay away," she repeated. "A man like Garth Endicott deserves undamaged merchandise."

She pivoted on her high heels, then stopped.

Garth stood in the doorway, unsmiling, blocking her exit. With slow deliberation he stepped into the room and closed the door, towering over her.

"Garth, I was just on my way out," she babbled. "It's so nice to see dear Kris back at—"

"Forget it, Sybil. We've discussed this already. You know what I'm talking about. I heard every word."

"But, Garth, I just—"

"Good-bye, Sybil." He opened the treatment room door and stared at her until she left.

Stunned, Kris listened to the click of Sybil's dainty heels disappearing down the hall.

For a moment they stood together in silence in the brightly lit room. Then Garth let the door swing shut and walked over to her. He stood there, saying nothing, until she forced herself to look up at him.

"Whatever you've planned to do tonight, Kris, cancel it. I'll be at your apartment at six. We're going to talk." Then he left.

Kris shut the apartment door and slumped against it. She closed her eyes, trying to calm down. Ever since Garth announced he was coming over tonight she'd been useless. She'd shelved the medication tally temporarily, planning to resume the count when anxiety wasn't short-circuiting her brain.

After all he'd put her through it made her angry to realize he could still upset her this way. She opened her eyes and surveyed the sunny apartment. He'd be here soon, but he wouldn't be staying long. She'd see to that.

Swallowing hard, she picked up the package she'd found leaning against the door when she arrived home and carried it to the kitchen. It was large and heavy, addressed to her in Grandma's careful, rounded script. Opening it would keep her mind off Garth's unwelcome visit and slow her escalating panic.

She slit the strapping tape open with a knife, pulled back the heavy brown wrapping paper, and lifted the cover from the box. Then she pushed aside a thick inner layer of crumpled tissue paper and caught her breath.

Inside was folded an exquisite quilt pieced in plain and patterned shades of blue, separated by tiny strips of pure white. A letter from Grandma rested on top. Kris set the letter aside and lifted out the quilt, spreading part of it open over one end of the table.

Though she hadn't quilted anything since high school, she recognized the design immediately—the Wedding Ring pattern, with stitches so tiny she had to bend close to see them. Again and again she ran her hand over the soft, strong fabric, marveling at the little pieces of angled blue cloth forming two entwined wedding rings.

She recognized a few scraps from old curtains and dresses made years ago, but most of the fabric she had never seen. The quilt was backed in a soft, pale blue, covered with enough delicate stitches to last her lifetime and longer.

Finally she sat down, her arms cradled in the warm folds of the half-open quilt, and opened Grandma's letter. It was short, neatly penned in blue ink on lined tablet paper, the kind Grandma saved for special occasions.

Dear Krissy,

This is the quilt I was at work on. And it is for you. I put the stitching more close together, to make it stronger. It's called Wedding Ring, on purpose. Because my prayer for you, Krissy, is to use this quilt. In the home you make with the man you love. Love him like I love you Krissy, but not so tight.

Chapter Nineteen

I loved you with fear, hoping to keep you from hurt. Looking back, I think I held you too tight to sadness. With your mother gone and your dad so poor and sad and all. I wanted better for you. So I'm saying follow your heart and let go of my tight strings, girl. I love you, and so I'm cutting you free.

Follow your heart, because God made you so special, Krissy. He made you for sunshine, like you give off to everyone yourself. So love big, Krissy. Love free. And when this quilt covers your marriage bed, remember it's the little stitches make the whole quilt strong. I love you.

Grandma

Kris almost couldn't read the last few sentences for her tears. Grandma was a woman of few words, and telling Kris she loved her had not been part of them. Grandma said more in this letter than she'd said in years.

Kris rested her head on the soft, half-folded quilt and closed her eyes. She'd always known Grandma loved her. But seeing it written in her dear hand had released an invisible steel band of doubt that had long imprisoned her. Warmed now by Grandma's words and the late afternoon sun across her shoulders, she drifted into a dreamless sleep.

Two hours later the persistent ring of the doorbell jarred her awake. She looked up, for a minute wondering where she was, but feeling more refreshed than she'd been in months.

Again the doorbell sounded, and then she remembered—Garth was coming over. She was still in her uniform, nothing was ready. But the panic she'd felt earlier was gone, and in its place was a sense of well-being she'd never experienced before.

I am with you always, Jesus promised. Always. In the horror of near-rape, and in loving a man who loved someone else. In being poor, and different, and scared. Always. And though she had no outward sign, Kris knew He'd been with her through all of what had happened. He was with her now, His healing already begun.

"Thank You, Father," she whispered. "I rest this evening in Your hands." She pushed the buzzer for Garth to come up.

She waited, listening as his steps grew louder, and opened the door before he knocked. Her heart beat fast, but around it remained a solid calm. Her eyes met his and held, telling her the old feelings were not gone. But underneath flowed a freedom, a relinquishment, a new peace. God was in control, and she could release Garth to Sybil with real joy.

"Hi," she smiled, closing the door behind him.

"Hi yourself," he answered, looking around the almost dark apartment. "Saving on electricity?"

She laughed. "I fell asleep."

"Do you always sleep in your uniform?"

"I was at the kitchen table. Grandma sent me the most beautiful quilt, and I sort of curled up over it. Sounds a little odd, I guess."

"Not really, considering. You've been pretty odd for the last few weeks, Kris." He seemed aggressive, as if he wanted to hurt her.

"I know," she replied. "Let's go into the kitchen. Would you like anything?"

"Most of all I want some questions answered—but a cup of tea would be good."

He sat down at the table as Kris turned on the kitchen light and started the tea kettle. He studied the quilt for a few seconds and whistled. "That thing's beautiful. Your grandmother made it for you?"

Kris nodded. "She's been working on it for months. It's called Wedding Ring." She stopped abruptly, wishing she hadn't volunteered that piece of information.

"You don't say." He sounded sarcastic.

Uneasy with the change in him tonight, Kris busied herself setting out mugs, tea bags, and ground coffee.

"Kris, please put that stuff away and sit down."

She stopped, a peppermint tea bag in hand, and glanced at him. He was leaning back, his white shirt open at the neck, a new firmness around his eyes. She pushed the tea bag into a mug of boiling water, handed it to him, and sat down.

"Okay," he said. "What's going on?"

She looked away. "I don't know what you mean."

"You know exactly what I mean. A couple weeks ago I kissed you over there." He leaned forward, pointing at the wicker couch angrily. "You kissed me back, Kris. And the days after that were beautiful. The next thing I know you're working fifteen hours at a time, walking alone at night in a dangerous area, and ending up—well, you of all people know the rest."

He sat straight, looking directly at her. "Every time I try to get close to you, you run. Just like always. And now you've turned into Florence Nightingale overnight. Nursing's great, Kris, but come on. I know that night meant as much to you as it did to me. What's going on?"

It was now or never. She cleared her throat, determined to be finished with this once and for all.

"It's no use, Garth. I saw you and Sybil together in the dining room." She shook her head, fighting back embarrassing hot tears. "I know you're really in love with her."

His tone of voice was incredulous, and a little bit angry. "Kris, what kind of man do you think I am? If I were in love with Sybil, what was I doing here kissing you two weeks ago?"

"Garth, please don't try to hide this from me any longer. You were engaged to her once before, and you're with her all the time. I've seen you leave the hospital with her almost every day." She bit her lower lip, struggling for the control she'd possessed only minutes before.

"Besides, I know she's so right for you. She has beautiful manners, she knows all about symphonies and opera and all that sort of thing. I'd be . . . I'm all wrong. I decided the best thing I could give you was to get out of your way." She met his eyes.

"Oh, Kris. Why couldn't you have trusted me just a little?" She felt his hand under her chin, turning her face toward his. He looked at her with transparent honesty. "Where did you get all these strange ideas about me, like this music thing? I don't care for most opera and, frankly, the symphony puts me to sleep. But I could listen to jazz and folk music all day."

Where had all those ideas come from? She tried to remember. "It's hard to put into words. I don't know."

"As for Sybil . . ." he said slowly. "She's a stubborn young lady, Kris. Always has been. Once she gets an idea into her head, there's no stopping her . . . until she discovers some new project. I used to consider her a good friend—after all, we've known each other all our lives—but it seems she's convinced herself I'm in love with her. She's done several things to prove it that I won't go into. You saw one of them this afternoon."

Her eyes never left his as he talked.

"Finally I had to tell her it was no good. I asked her to leave me alone, Kris. That's what I was telling her up in the dining room when you saw us. And as for leaving the hospital with her . . . she usually manages to walk out the door when I do, but you know where I go each afternoon—to the Y."

Her mind raced. If he were telling the truth, then everything she'd seen, everything she'd thought, everything she'd gone through she'd brought on herself. And if he didn't love Sybil, then. . . .

Chapter Nineteen

"But Kris, let's forget about Sybil. I want to talk about you. What do you mean, you're all wrong? What makes you think you're so different from other people?"

She felt cornered, frightened, desperate for somewhere to hide. Then her fragile dam of feelings burst open, and the words flooded out.

"I'm different because my family's different," she snapped. "Garth, when I was little we were worse than poor. I wore secondhand shoes and dresses Grandma made from ugly sale material. I always got teased about how I looked, and about my wild hair. I couldn't even be a cheerleader because they knew my family couldn't afford the uniform." She hung her head.

"What else, darling?" he whispered.

She didn't hear him. "I have two memories of when I was really little. One was when a black station wagon drove away with my mother's body in it, covered with a blanket. I was supposed to be in my room, but I hid behind the door and peeked out." Her voice caught.

"The other was when two horrible women brought Christmas food to us in boxes. They stared at everything in our dingy little house and whispered the whole time." She was crying now. "They said how terrible it was that some people let themselves live this way. I was hiding behind my favorite old chair . . . my safe chair . . . they didn't know I was there. But I heard them! I hated them, and their stuck-up ways and fake smiles!"

She tossed her hair back, ignoring her tears. "They were right about one thing, though. We were different. The whole time I was growing up it never changed. We were the poorest family in town. Everyone gave us their left-overs, and it made them feel good. We never had money for pictures or vacations or anything—I have seven snapshots from my whole childhood.

"I got into college on a scholarship, and wanted more

than anything to be a nurse. I studied day and night, and I made it. But always in my mind I'm so ashamed, thinking back to that safe old chair and those awful ladies and wanting to hide and never, ever come out." She sobbed uncontrollably.

The next thing she knew Garth was pulling her to her feet, wrapping her in his arms, holding her against him. Slowly her crying lessened, and she groped for a handkerchief. He handed her a paper napkin and she blew her nose.

"I'm sorry. I didn't mean to unload all that."

"I asked, my darling. It had to come out."

This time she heard. She looked up, her eyes red from crying, the paper napkin crumpled in her fist.

"Kris," he said, his voice overflowing with tenderness. "Kris, you're still hiding behind the safe chair. But it's you I'm looking for. I don't even see that living room. I see the way you care for children, and your beautiful curly hair, and your home, and your wonderful laughter. I'm holding out my hand to you, my beloved." He stroked her hair. "I know what's all around you, how ugly it is, how much it hurts. God made you so sensitive, and you feel so much. Kris, reach for my hand. Walk out from behind that old chair. Walk out with me."

"I want to, but. . . ."

He pointed to the chair she'd been sitting in. "Would you please sit down for a minute? There's something I don't think you understand yet." He pulled out his chair and sat across from her.

She did as he said, still sniffling but wanting to listen, to soak up the magic in his voice and words.

"Kris," he said, leaning toward her, "do you remember when you first told me about the Lord, you said He was with us in everything? That He accepts us exactly the way we are? That He promised never to leave us?"

"Yes," she answered softly.

"Then that kind of love, Jesus' love, is our model, isn't it?"

"Yes."

He covered her hands with his. "That's the love I have for you, Kris. I want to be with you whatever comes, exactly the way you are." His huge hand brushed against her cheek and moved back, stroking her hair. "Kris, I love you. I think I've loved you since I first saw you."

She reached out to him in silent answer. Garth stood again and pulled her to her feet, drawing her head to his shoulder. They stood together in the silence.

Kris closed her eyes, feeling the broad strength of him, knowing she was safe. He was offering his love to her free of all conditions. She didn't have to do anything or be anything or prove anything. He loved her exactly as she was.

He pulled back a few inches and tilted her face to his. "Our love is a gift, Kris, straight from God's hand. If we refuse it, we're turning away from what He's planned for us. I love you, and I'll never be complete without you beside me." He looked down at her, his eyes probing hers, waiting for her answer.

She thought of the quilt, still half unfolded on one end of the pine table, and of Grandma's letter. Grandma said not to hold back—to love free, love big, to follow her heart. Kris looked up at Garth, Grandma's words echoing in her mind.

She smiled through her tears, filled with a new freeing joy. "Oh, Garth, I do love you!" she whispered, awed by the sound of the words she'd never allowed herself to say. "I'll need time to heal, time to learn to trust. But I've loved you for so long." Her words were cut short as his lips closed over hers.

At last he pulled away, looking down at her with a

sweetness she would carry forever in her memory. "You're off tomorrow, aren't you?"

"Yes."

"I'll pick you up in the morning then. Is eight o'clock too early?"

She shook her head. "Where are we going?"

"That, my darling, is a surprise. Kris, I love you so much."

This time it was she who reached out, circled his neck with her arms, and pulled him to her.

THE STEEL TOWERS OF THE Golden Gate Bridge soared above them as they sped north. Like her heart, they stretched heavenward in praise to God. Behind them the steep hills of San Francisco, dotted with buildings of every age and size, receded in the distance. Below rippled the Bay's deep, silver-gray waters, guarding the city's entrance. Ahead, backlit by the blue sky of early morning, beckoned the sloping hills of Marin County.

Kris snuggled sideways into her seat, her left hand nestled against Garth's shoulder. "Now tell me," she coaxed. "Where are we going?"

"To one of my favorite places . . . a place almost as beautiful as you."

They left the majestic bridge behind them as the car headed up a narrow, winding road. Behind them shimmered the ocean, whitecaps sparkling in the sun. Turning west onto Highway One, the car entered Muir Woods, skirted the brooding splendor of Mt. Tamalpais, and continued north for several miles.

Garth turned onto an unpaved area and stopped the car near the edge of a steep cliff.

"Garth," Kris whispered, "this is magnificent."

He circled the car to open her door, and with his arm

tight around her waist led her to the cliff's edge. She traced the endless expanse of ocean to its disappearance on the horizon, her hair buffeted by the capricious wind. On every side the air's whispered song drifted through the massive, swaying redwoods. The earth, carpeted with dry, gold-brown grass, rippled before the wind's unseen force.

Kris leaned against him, soaking up the power and wonder of this place.

"I've come here for years," he said after several minutes. "To think, and make plans, and just absorb the beauty. This is where I always got my strength. But when we met, and you told me about the Lord, it was as if He gathered this place together, and poured it into you." His arm tightened around her. "It's hard to put into words," he said slowly. "But I don't need this spot anymore. Because instead of this, God gave me the gift of you."

He faced her, his eyes as gold and green as the trees and grass surrounding them. With his massive hands he tipped her face to his. "I love you, my darling . . . and I want you to be my wife. Will you marry me, Kris?"

Her heart thrilled with a happiness she'd waited for all her life. She reached up to him, whole and complete in the miracle of his love.